Death
Is
Semisweet

Also by Lou Jane Temple

Death
Is
Semisweet

LOU JANE TEMPLE

ST. MARTIN'S MINOTAUR ✽ NEW YORK

ISBN 0-312-30122-7

For

Charlene Welling and Mary Simpson,

who are always there through thick and thin

Death
Is
Semisweet

Miracle Whip Chocolate Cake

2 cups flour
1 cup sugar
pinch salt
1 tsp. baking soda
4 T. cocoa
1 cup cold water
1 cup Miracle Whip
1 tsp. vanilla

This is a standard Midwestern housewife recipe that was probably printed on the Miracle Whip jar at some time. Bob Bond, a friend of mine, got it from his mother, Evelyn, in Joplin, Missouri.

Combine all dry ingredients. Mix well. Add all liquids and mix to combine. Bake at 350 degrees for 30 minutes. Frost with Hershey's chocolate frosting.

Hershey's Chocolate Frosting

1 stick butter
⅔ cup cocoa
3 cups powdered sugar
⅓ cup milk
1 tsp. vanilla

Melt butter. Stir in cocoa. Alternate adding powdered
sugar and milk, beating until smooth with each addition.
Add more milk if needed to obtain spreading consistency.
Stir in vanilla.

One

Heaven Lee woke with a start. Sections of the *Kansas City Star* and the *New York Times* Sunday papers were on her chest, on the bed, on the floor. She stretched and looked around contentedly, then pulled a variety of pillows toward her and arranged them as a back rest, organizing the scattered papers into two piles, separating the *Times* from the *Star*. It was 10:30 on Sunday morning and she was still in bed.

Sunday was the only day Café Heaven was closed so it was the only day of the week staying in bed late with the paper was a possibility. She had the Kansas City paper delivered every day but the *New York Times* only on Sunday. She didn't have enough time to read two newspapers every morning. Half the time she didn't have time to read one in the morning, reading the *Star* when she got home from the restaurant late at night. Today she'd gotten through the arts and editorial sections before dozing off again. Lazy Sundays didn't come around too often.

Heaven hopped out of bed and went downstairs for another cup of coffee. She'd gotten up with Hank Wing, had her first cup then. Hank had gone around the corner to spend some time with his mother and attend mass at Holy Rosary Catholic Church with her. Heaven was never invited on these outings. She wasn't Catholic and Hank's mother didn't approve of her, a fact of life Hank accepted better than Heaven did.

Heaven's home in the Columbus Park district of Kansas City was a storefront. The first floor was one big commercial kitchen, laundry room, dining room and entertaining area, with lots of storage places for foodstuffs and dishes and platters and baskets and wine glasses. Before Heaven opened the restaurant, she'd run a catering business out of this floor.

She poured more coffee and also got a Diet Coke out of the big reach-in refrigerator, anticipating the move to a cold form of caffeine soon. She spotted a big chunk of chocolate sheet cake in the refrigerator and added it to her tray. She returned to the bed upstairs, took a bite of cake and followed it with coffee. Then she grabbed the phone from the bedside table.

She dialed and when someone answered, broke into a big smile. "Hi, honey, it's your mom."

"Mom, I'm so glad you called. What are you doing?" The voice on the other end of the line was hesitant, reserved. It was Iris, Heaven's daughter. Iris had finished her last year at Oxford and was still living in England with her father, the rock musician Dennis McGuinne. She was launching herself as a writer and she was in love.

"I have the day off and I'm still in bed. It's absolutely glorious. Hank went to church with his mom and I made coffee and got back in bed. In fact, I've already had my first nap."

"Why don't you just stay there all day. I'm sure Hank will come back and join you," Iris said, teasing, then felt embarrassed about making a sexual crack to her mom. She was glad her mother couldn't see her turning red.

Heaven wasn't going to bite. "I can't stay in bed because I have a brunch date with Stephanie Simpson. She's going to teach me about chocolate. But then I'm coming home and staying here. It's probably the last time this month I'll get to do this. It's been busy at the restaurant since Thanksgiving and even though we're not open on Sundays, it seems like I have stuff to do on Sundays the rest of the month. When will you be home?"

Iris had been firm last year when she explained to her mother that after college, she wasn't coming back to live in Kansas City. It had been rough to accept, but Heaven couldn't blame her daughter. Iris had a world view. Heaven just wanted her to remember where her emotional "home" was. After all, Iris had grown up in Kansas City, moving to Cambridge and her father only for her college years. The last four years had been good for Iris and Dennis, or so they both said. Heaven had accepted the separation until this year, when it led to Iris falling in love with a man of whom Heaven was afraid.

"Well, I'm coming on the 20th and today is the 10th, so only ten more days," Iris said, still with the hesitation in her voice. "I'm really looking forward to it, Mom."

"Oh, honey, so am I. I told my brother we'd come out to the farm on Christmas Day, but Christmas Eve we'll have a get-together here, or at the restaurant, I'm not sure where yet. . . ."

"Mom," Iris said more sharply than she'd meant to, cutting off her mother's chattering mid-stream. "Stuart is coming with me."

Silence for at least ten seconds.

5

"Mom, are you still there?"

"Gosh, Iris, I would think Mr. Watts would want to spend Christmas with some of his children. How about the ones that are older than you? Doesn't he even have a grandchild?" Heaven's voice dripped with sarcasm.

"Mother, I thought we'd gotten to the point where you accept that I love this man. Now I've tried to respect your wishes, and Dad's too, as far as that goes, and not move in with him. But he's coming with me to Kansas City and that's that."

Silence again, but only for a couple of seconds, while Heaven figured out her next move. "Well, then, shall I book him a room at the Fairmont Hotel?" she asked archly, knowing she was fighting a losing battle.

This time there was a good solid pause on the *other* end of the line.

Heaven didn't want this to become a battle royale but the idea of that aging rock star and her daughter sharing her daughter's childhood bedroom was pretty hard to take.

"Why is it just fine for you to have a boyfriend just a few years older than I am, but I can't have a boyfriend in your age category?" Iris asked bluntly.

"Hank is a perfectly respectable doctor, thank you very much. Stuart Watts, on the other hand, is the most flagrant violator of every rule in the book and then some. He makes your father's escapades look tame."

"He used to act like that but he doesn't now. Father too. Everyone has a past, Mother," Iris said with a very sharp edge to her voice. "Do you want me to start in on yours?"

"No, but—"

Iris broke in before her mother said something that really made her mad. So far the conversation had been entirely predictable. "Good. Then let's just discuss what a wonderful time we're all going to have. Stuart will fly in with me, stay at our house until the 24th, then fly to San Francisco where, yes, like the devoted father and grandfather he is, he will have Christmas with his daughter Lana and her husband and his darling granddaughter, Lucretia, who will be one year old the day after Christmas. His son Webb, the director, will come up from LA. His other daughter, the older one, you know, the one that's actually thirty, is doing some relief work in Ecuador or someplace. He'll see her later. Are you still paying attention?"

"Like a teacher's pet," Heaven snapped.

"Then Stuart will come back to Kansas City so we can spend New Year's Eve together. He wanted to go to Bali for New Year's but I said it would be more fun to be with you, that you always had something wild going on at the restaurant and then everyone came over to our house and danced and carried on until dawn. So we'll go to Bali on the third or fourth of January. So there."

"Talk about having your cake and eating it too," Heaven cracked, trying to pout but not really having the heart for it. "When do you have time to write, missy? What with Kansas City in December and Bali in January. What happens in February, a space shuttle trip?"

Iris, relieved the boyfriend issue had been supplanted with the when-are-you-going-to-get-a-real-job issue, ignored the travel schedule jab. "I have a new piece that will be in *Tattler* next month. You remember I covered Iris Murdoch's memorial service at school? I wrote about how you and Dad had named me after her and how it had had a profound effect on my life and about meeting her and all."

7

"Where is my copy of the article? I want to have it bronzed," Heaven said, only half joking.

"I'll bring one to Kansas City if it's out. I can't believe it takes two weeks for the Brit magazines to get there. But my next piece will be easy for you to go buy for yourself. It's going to be in *Rolling Stone*," Iris said with triumph.

Heaven didn't want to spoil Iris's moment by saying something mean like, of course *Rolling Stone* would give the daughter of Dennis McGuinne a shot at writing something. They both knew that was how the world worked. She also knew Iris had the talent to do a good job and get the second assignment on merit. "Congratulations, honey. What are you writing about?"

"I'm going on tour with two new English bands, kind of retro punk with some world beat thrown in. I know it sounds like a bizarre combination but actually it's quite brilliant. I'll do the on-the-road piece. Then I get to do a Jazz in Paris piece, because of the Kansas City connection, by the way. I may need your help on that, since you know more about jazz than I do and you helped with that big jazz party last spring."

Heaven looked at the clock. It was a little past eleven and she had to meet Stephanie Simpson on the Plaza at noon. "We'll look up Jim Dittmar when you get here. He'll know what's going on if he isn't over in Paris playing gigs himself."

"Isn't that the piano player you thought was a jewel thief, Mom?"

"It's his shifty friends that led me to that conclusion. You see, just another reason not to get involved with a musician. Bye, honey. I'm going out to shop for twin beds for your room now. I'll talk to you next week."

"Mother!" Iris thought her mom was kidding about the beds but you could never be sure.

"I really am looking forward to you being home for Christmas, and old what's-his-name, too. I'm hanging up now," Heaven said and she did.

Heaven raced for the shower and after a good ten minutes of various shampoos and antioxidant scrubs and loofah rubs, she was positively a new woman. Even though she'd rinsed off in the shower when she got home from work the night before, her hair had still smelled like a pu-pu platter of the cafe's menu selections, at least to her. She was very sensitive to food smells on her clothes and hair and body. Hank always said she just smelled like someone who worked around food and that he liked it. Hank was always so positive.

Now came the task of finding something clean to wear. Laundry was definitely on the agenda for the afternoon. Heaven had purchased new underwear last week, instead of doing laundry. She had to face the music this week. Pulling a big black cashmere turtleneck sweater out of a drawer, her only expensive sweater, she found a pair of ribbed leggings, some red cowboy boots to celebrate the season, and she was set, except for her hair, which was drying in an unruly red mop. She spent a few minutes with the hair dryer, then decided to go all the way and put on lipstick and mascara. It was during this last delicate procedure that a crash from the first floor made her blink, causing a deposit of black gunk on her face under the lashes. "Damn," Heaven exclaimed.

"Heaven, are you all right?" Hank yelled from the kitchen. "And if you are, can you come help me?"

"Just a second," Heaven yelled as she quickly repaired the damage she'd done to her face. She'd just never really gotten the hang of the makeup thing. It was a good thing too, as she'd chosen a career that required a clean face most of the time. Makeup just melted in a hot professional-kitchen situation.

Heaven grabbed a black leather jacket and an orange wool scarf and headed downstairs.

"You look nice. Very festive," Hank said as he surveyed her, then looked back at the problem. A giant Christmas tree was wedged half in the door, half out in the garage. "I think this is a two-man job," Hank said. "I'll go out in the garage and manage the heavy end if you'll pull on the top."

Heaven looked at the tree with mixed feelings. "It looks magnificent. It's probably at least twenty or thirty years old. And now it's dead so we can have a place to put our stupid Christmas presents." She stood with her hands on her hips and gave one stomp with a red cow-boy boot.

Hank rolled his eyes and put his hands on Heaven's shoulders, pulling her close. He had on a beautiful vin-tage gabardine overcoat from the 1950s, gray, and car-amel colored leather gloves that looked vintage but weren't, the kind with the stitching on the outside. His long black hair was loose on his shoulders. "We've been through this for the last four years. You agonize over whether or not to get a tree and then at the last minute you want one and we end up with some freak of nature with branches on only one side, like the one last year. I decided to go to the city market while there was still a good selection and get the kind of tree you should have—and magnificent is the word for it, just like you." He had been addressing her like the slow girl in the class. Now he bent down and kissed her.

Had it really been four years that Hank had been

around at Christmas? That couldn't possibly be right. "Doesn't this killing of trees bother your ancient Buddhist sensibilities?" she asked, pulling out of the embrace reluctantly.

Hank laughed and let go of her, heading for another route to the garage through the front door, since he couldn't get back out the way he came in. "Even though I'm from Vietnam, I was raised a Catholic, remember. We love to celebrate Christmas. It's little Jesus' birthday." He stopped and turned back to Heaven. "Think about the food that you serve in your restaurant. It was raised for a purpose. The cattle, the pigs, the carrots, the lettuce, even the grains. It was all raised to be consumed, to be fuel for another life-form. These Christmas trees were raised on a farm, just like wheat. They were raised to be consumed. Just because they take longer to get to harvest, doesn't mean their purpose on earth wasn't clear from the start."

Heaven gave up. "Then let's get the damn thing in here. I'm supposed to be on the Plaza in ten minutes."

Hank grinned. "I'll get the decorations out of the basement while you're gone. Then tonight, we'll trim the tree, just the two of us."

"How corny," Heaven said, and rolled her eyes at Hank. In truth, she could hardly wait.

Chocolate Bread Pudding

1 qt. half and half
2 cups heavy cream
1 cup sugar
7 eggs, beaten
6 egg yolks, beaten
1 tsp. vanilla extract
6 oz. semisweet chocolate chips
1 loaf thin sliced white bread

My friend, professional pastry chef Susan Welling Sanchez, shared this recipe as well as the flourless torte in the next chapter. They are the best examples of two chocolate standards I've ever tasted.

Scald the half and half and cream with the sugar. Temper this into the combined beaten eggs and yolks like this: Mix a small amount of the hot cream mixture into the beaten eggs and yolks and then slowly combine the eggs and all the cream. Add vanilla and chocolate chips. The hot cream will melt the chocolate slightly.

Slice the bread in two on the diagonal. Arrange sliced triangles in a deep baking dish. Strain the custard with a wire mesh strainer over the bread slices. Put the baking dish in another pan containing enough water to reach about half way up the sides of the baking dish, a bain marie, at 325 degrees for 45 minutes or until the custard is firm.

Two

Everywhere you looked, there was another Santa. Dozens of them were trooping along in front of the café. Some of them had on the typical Santa Claus costume: red suit, white fur trim, black belt, freshly groomed white beard and portly tummy. But others were trying a cutting-edge approach. There were red tights instead of trousers, a tie-dyed tunic, one Santa with dread locks, and several with bizarre accessories like rhinestone belts, small dogs with Santa hats, and one bratty child dressed up as an elf who stuck her tongue out at Heaven and Stephanie Simpson inside the restaurant as she marched past outside.

The Plaza, a faux Spanish shopping center built in the 1920s and '30s, was Kansas City's pride and joy. Long brick buildings with red tile roofs and fronted with elaborate statuary housed Gap and Barnes and Noble stores. There were European streetlights and a slightly shorter rendition of the Tower of Seville, Spain, the sister city of Kansas City. The Plaza was known nationwide for its elaborate Christmas decorations, which involved outlining every building for several blocks with lights. This year, that obviously wasn't enough. The Plaza seemed to be recruiting Santas by the dozens.

"I'm stuffed," Stephanie moaned as she pushed back her plate. "I can't believe I ordered dessert after corned beef hash."

Heaven had finished her own order, eggs Benedict. She took her fork and pointed it at Stephanie's plate. "You've always had a sweet tooth and you never put on a pound, you dog. Maybe I'll just have a bite of this chocolate bread pudding. So go on with your tale. Your new boutique, gourmet, fancy-schmancy chocolate shop is doing great, you're so tired you can't move because this is your first Christmas with a retail business. By the way, I've being meaning to ask you this and I always forget: Why did you decide to do this?"

Stephanie paused with her coffee cup halfway to her mouth. She thought better of it, put down the cup and picked up her champagne glass instead. She sipped her mimosa and shook her head. "Earth to Heaven, so to speak. I got dumped by my dog of a husband, remember? Even with a hefty financial punishment for breaking my heart . . ."

"And running off with his receptionist," Heaven added.

"Yes, let's not forget that. It couldn't be his assistant or a paralegal, God forbid. It had to be the receptionist, not that it isn't a perfectly good job. Men really do go for the most geographically available and the easiest, don't they?"

"What they can reach out and grab," Heaven quipped. "No, I realize you probably couldn't make a living just doing food styling here in Kansas City. But when faced with the inevitability of having to get a real job, why did you choose opening a chocolate shop?"

"The blimp," Stephanie said, waving toward outside. A large pink blimp was floating over the Plaza, as large as the Goodyear blimp only shocking pink. It was painted, "Season's Greetings from Foster's Chocolates" on one side and "Foster's Chocolates 50 Year Anniversary" on the other.

"Yeah," Heaven said, not looking up. "I've seen it the last couple of days. It hovered over 39th street Friday at rush hour. What does Foster's blimp have to do with you opening a chocolate shop?"

"Oh, I forget you didn't grow up here, Heaven. I'm a member of the family that owns the number one boxed chocolate candy company in the country. The poor side of the family, as luck would have it."

"Foster's?" Heaven finally looked out the front glass doors of the Classic Cup, her friend Charlene Welling's restaurant. The tail end of the blimp gracefully disappeared from view.

"Celebrating their fiftieth year," Stephanie said with an affirmative nod.

"Well, hell then, why didn't you go to work for your family if you wanted to be in the chocolate business?"

Stephanie was a petite blond fashion plate. Known for her incredible wardrobe and her red nails before the divorce, she now looked down at hands with dozens of little nicks and scrapes on them. No nail polish. Hardly even any nails, as Stephanie was using her hands to dip chocolates, bake brownies and clean out espresso machines. She studied her disastrous cuticles a split-second more, then looked up at Heaven and smiled wanly. "Here's the short version. The long version we don't have time for until Christmas is over. When the first snow falls in January, we'll get drunk and I'll have a ball feeling sorry for myself, telling you not only how my mother was swindled out of a fortune, but how my husband hid his assets in the Cayman Islands. I'm a second-generation patsy. The short version of my mother's disaster is, there were five children in my mother's family, the Foster family."

"Did your mom grow up here in Kansas City?"

"Oh, yes. Foster's Chocolate is a hometown company. It was started by my grandfather after the war. At first their products were sold exclusively in a department store downtown. I'm not sure which one. In those days I think the company did little more than feed my grandfather's five kids, who were mostly already teenagers. Ten years passed and my mother's oldest brother, Harold Foster, Jr., got involved with his dad's company; it turned out he really had a head for business. The company was doing better. But none of the other kids knew that. Now here it comes, Heaven, pay attention."

"Someone is going to get screwed," Heaven said, as she polished off the last bite of Stephanie's bread pudding.

"My grandfather died of a heart attack. My mother's two older brothers, who are both working in the business by now, go to the two girls and the youngest child, my uncle David, and say, look, you two girls are married; David, you're in college. We want to buy your shares of the company because that's the only way we can see anyone will make a living out of this place, if the pie is divided only two ways. We'll buy Mom's shares too, and of course, make sure if her money runs out that she has a house and everything she needs, and David, we'll also pay your college expenses. So they bought the three younger kids out for a pittance and then took the company public and made a fortune for themselves."

"Wow, they were ahead of their time with the corporate greed thing," Heaven observed. "That's a very 1990s kind of a story. Was your mom pissed?"

"Well, as you can guess, it has divided the family. We don't go over to Junior's big old mansion for a festive evening of Christmas carols and eggnog, I can tell you that. My dad blames himself, of course, for not seeing it coming. But my dad is a kindly family doctor and doesn't have a dishonest bone in his body."

"Did your grandmother get evicted from the family home by the two evil brothers? That would really give this story a nice little kick," Heaven said, cynical as always.

"Oh, the family home was too small for Junior and Claude to bother with, although my grandmother has a perfectly good fake Tudor near Ward Parkway, similar to mine. The brothers moved over to Mission Hills as fast as they could. No, Nana is in her late eighties and going strong in her own home, with help of course. But it has made a difference in her relationship with my mother and Aunt Carol and Uncle David. They think she should have stuck up for them more. I think she didn't understand a thing about the business but now knows what side her bread is buttered on and doesn't want to die in the poor house. Not that she would. My mother would always make sure she was taken care of. So would my aunt and uncle. But the brothers have power over her, financially. I think that would be scary at her age."

Heaven put up her hand to get the waiter's attention. "I'm buying brunch because you're going to let me tag around and watch you with the chocolates. We haven't even gotten around to why I need your expertise. This whole Foster's drama is fascinating. I have two more questions, then I know you want to go back around the corner to your shop."

Stephanie grinned at her friend and started applying lipstick and other beauty aids she'd pulled out of a huge purse. She hadn't changed completely. "Oh, the Foster family is just like a story from *Dallas*, the old TV show, believe me. Question number one?"

"What about your aunt and uncle? Do they live in Kansas City? I bet your uncle was pissed to be cheated like one of the girls."

Stephanie snapped her mirrored compact shut. "You know, I'd never thought of it like that. David's gay. He's a professor at Duke or somewhere like that. I rarely see him but maybe he lost that good old male bloodlust along with his company shares. My aunt Carol lives right out in Independence. She and her husband retired a couple of years ago, bought one of those motor homes, and now they travel around. I don't think Carol or my mom give it much thought anymore. It turned out their husbands were good providers, not that that makes it okay. Then there's my cousin, but that's another story. Enough family history. Question two?"

Heaven was signing the credit card receipt when a sharp retort sounded from outside. The Plaza was noisy with tourists and Salvation Army bell ringers and Christmas carols being piped outside all over the area but this sound cut through all the normal shopping sounds. *Crack.* There it was again. *Crack.* And again. It sounded like gunfire. Heaven looked around and saw Charlene Welling leave the hostess desk and head for the door, concern on her face. "Did you hear that?" Heaven asked.

Stephanie got up and slipped her coat on, a gorgeous red wool number that set off her blond hair. She looked out the glass doors that lined the front of the restaurant. "Something's going on because people are running down the street," she said, pointing outside. "I hope my chocolate shop hasn't been robbed or isn't on fire or anything."

Heaven and Stephanie hurried to the door. Now the crowd was running in the opposite direction, looking behind them fearfully. The inordinate number of Santas gave the whole crowd a surrealistic look. Children were shrieking and clutching their parents.

Heaven and Stephanie stepped outside just in time to see the Foster's Chocolate blimp come crashing into the Plaza, its giant pink mass getting hung up on the three-quarters-size replica of the Seville Tower that was a centerpiece of the shopping center. There it swayed, looking like the deflated Claes Oldenburg sculpture of a blimp instead of the real thing.

Suddenly a man dropped like dead weight out of the cockpit to the ground.

Sergeant Bonnie Weber of the Kansas City, Missouri, Police Department sat on a stool in the back room of the Chocolate Queen, eating a chocolate truffle and drinking espresso. Heaven was there too, holding a huge hunk of chocolate-covered popcorn that looked like a dirty, uneven popcorn ball. She had decided on the ladylike approach to eating it and was breaking off chunks and popping them in her mouth, as opposed to just biting into it like an apple. Stephanie was assembling a gift basket for a customer.

"I can't believe you two knew that was the sound of a high-powered rifle going off," Bonnie said.

Heaven tossed her head, getting ready to brag, then

thought better of it. "Well, maybe not exactly a high-powered rifle, but it was definitely gunshots, that part was plain. You know, Bonnie, after all the school shootings and workplace massacres, if you think you hear gunshots, it really gets your attention. Who knows, you may have time to hide. We were sittings ducks up there in the front of the Classic Cup, what with all that glass."

Stephanie had been subdued since the accident. "I thought my shop was being robbed, of course. I never would have guessed it was a sharpshooter taking out the pilot of the Foster blimp. That's too outrageous." She sounded as if she still couldn't believe what she'd seen.

"Well, it is a homicide, and that's why I'm here, of course," Bonnie said as she reached for another truffle. "But it remains to be seen if the shooter was actually aiming for the pilot or just shooting at the blimp in general and hit the pilot. Either way it was a lucky shot. I think the first two shots hit the body of the blimp, the gas started rushing out, forcing the blimp down, and the pilot leaned close to the window to see what the hell was going on and put himself in harm's way, poor guy."

"At least they don't burst into a ball of flames anymore," Heaven said. "That could have been a real disaster, especially if it hadn't gotten caught up on the tower and had landed in the middle of the Christmas shoppers."

"You have such a vivid imagination. What does your imagination think the motive for this little criminal act might be?" Bonnie asked.

Heaven shook her head. "Bonnie, what a question. You want a motive? More people get killed nowadays just for being in the wrong place at the wrong time than used to get killed on purpose. Maybe someone didn't like pink. Maybe they were practicing up to go into their place of employment tomorrow and mow down their fellow workers. How about that?"

Bonnie ignored her friend's all-too-true commentary on homicide today. Brilliant deductive reasoning didn't get you anywhere anymore. Not when random violence and family troubles gave her most of her customers. "Well, thanks to Stephanie, I do know more about Foster's Chocolates than I did when I arrived on the scene. What do think, Stephanie, did your mom and your aunt Carol pick off the Foster's blimp?"

Stephanie smiled uneasily, knowing that Bonnie would probably check out her family. She was good at her job. "No, if those two were going to take revenge, they'd go right to my two brothers. They wouldn't mess around with some weird dirigible and the pilot," Stephanie said with a little laugh. "My mother, however, would have to use those heavy loaves of bread she bakes as weapons. Mom doesn't believe in firearms. She wouldn't allow a gun in the house and my dad was fine with that."

Heaven looked at her watch. "It's four and when I called and said I'd be late, I promised I'd be home around four. Hank and I are going to decorate the Christmas tree tonight."

The moment the words were out of her mouth she knew she'd made a mistake. Both Bonnie and Stephanie whooped and whistled and made disparaging remarks about domestic bliss. Heaven actually knew that they both liked Hank and they couldn't understand why she couldn't just relax and enjoy the good fortune of having a really nice boyfriend. Heaven remained edgy about the whole thing. Her history of relationships with men wasn't that good.

As she put on her coat and ate a chocolate-covered

almond, she remembered. "Steph, after all this, I forgot to tell you why I wanted to know more about chocolate. And now that I know you're really a dispossessed heir to the Foster's fortune, you may not want to help."

"Why?" both women asked at more or less the same time.

"To celebrate this big anniversary, Foster's asked all these chefs from around the country to create a chocolate dessert with Foster's chocolate. I'm one of them. I guess they'll do a cookbook or something. They're having a big chocolate party with all the chefs' dishes on New Year's Eve at the Fairmont."

Stephanie sniffed. "I could care less how they celebrate their damn anniversary. Come over here Tuesday morning and I'll put you to work."

"Thanks. What an eventful Sunday on the Plaza." Heaven hugged Stephanie, who was trying to tie a big bow on the gift basket and couldn't hug back. "Bonnie, lend her your finger. Good luck with the shooter," she said as she went out the door.

Bonnie Weber went over to help Stephanie with her bow. Maybe there was something that Stephanie hadn't told her the first time, some little fact that she'd overlooked. "Okay, buddy, just go through the Foster family feud one more time."

"Why don't they?" Hank asked. He was up on a ladder, stringing the lights at the top of the tree.

Heaven was sitting on the floor, surrounded by Christmas ornaments. She had two big boxes that she was working out of and there were dozens of smaller boxes inside the big boxes that contained different categories of decorations. She opened a box and carefully unwrapped an old German Santa ornament, and instantly she was lost in memories.

Heaven's mother had carried on an antique business in the barn of their farm near Alma, Kansas, and through her, Heaven got interested in collecting back when she was still called Katy O'Malley.

Heaven had been collecting Christmas ornaments since she was a child. At estate auctions she attended with her mom, she had discovered at an early age that Christmas ornaments were always tucked away in boxes from the deceased's basement. Heaven would find a good box and then ask her folks to bid on it when the time came.

Heaven's whole house was full of interesting collections: antique quilts and beautiful antique glassware and dishes that Heaven had used in her catering business. Heaven herself had had a business buying and selling jukeboxes when she was a teenager. There was a prize Wurlitzer right across the room.

"Heaven, did you hear me?" Hank had turned from the tree to see what was going on.

Heaven was miles and years away. She looked down at the Santa in her hand. "I was just thinking about the sale where I got this ornament. It was in Concordia, Kansas; the family had come from Germany originally and how they ever brought these glass Christmas ornaments all the way to Kansas I don't know, but they had dozens of beautiful, elaborate ones. Mom bid on them for me and I got four of the really good ones. I still have three. I dropped the fourth one and broke it a few years ago and cried like a baby about it."

"How old were you when you got that Santa?"

"I guess about nine or ten," Heaven said, back in the

real world now, placing the Santa carefully on the coffee table in front of her.

Hank climbed off the stepladder and came over and sat on the couch behind Heaven. He put his arm on her shoulder. "I think you're missing your parents right now."

Heaven looked up at Hank and smiled. "They've been dead more than twenty years but it just seems like yesterday I was out there in Kansas, hanging out with them, going to auctions, being a kid. Yes, Christmas is definitely a time I miss them. I wish they'd met Iris," she said, hating herself for being so sentimental.

Hank got up and picked up the electrical cord. "Well, this is the moment of truth. I will now plug in the lights." He bowed formally as if he were the ringmaster at a circus.

After much conferring, Heaven and Hank had decided to go with all-white lights this year, the small Italian variety. They had several choices at hand, including the antique bubble lights that Heaven loved but that made Hank nervous. Two years ago in the neighborhood, a Christmas-tree fire burned down a house, displacing a Viet family that Hank knew. Heaven was willing to give up the bubble lights this year so Hank wouldn't get up several times a night to make sure the tree wasn't on fire, as he'd done last year, even though the lights were completely unplugged at bed time. Hank was usually so calm and logical his nervousness about Christmas lights endeared him to Heaven even more.

When Hank plugged in the lights the tree was beautiful, the rows of lights orderly but not perfect and anal retentive. It was just the way Heaven would do them if she had the patience to do them, which she didn't, but

Hank did. They had decided against twinkling, at least for now.

"Hurrah," Heaven said, and clapped her hands. "We already have the best Christmas tree in town and it doesn't have an ornament on it. Now I'm going to stop daydreaming and fly into action." She walked over to Hank and slipped her arms around his neck. "This really is much better than the one-sided tree of last year. Thank you."

"You're welcome," Hank said. "Now will you answer my question of ten minutes ago, which was, 'Why don't blimps burst into flames any more?' "

Heaven was already busy at work on the tree, placing an ornament, then standing back and squinting at it, then moving the ornament a hair one way or the other. "Well, it still could if you hit the fuel tank. They have to have some kind of fuel to get around. The gas just fills up the blimp part, makes it lighter than air, it doesn't power it. But the sniper didn't hit the fuel tank. He tore some holes in the body of the blimp and the gas escaped and that made it fall. And of course the sniper also killed the pilot, who might have been able to make a better landing if he'd been, you know . . . ."

"Alive?"

"Yeah, that," Heaven said, engrossed in her job. "The famous fire one, the Hindenburg, was filled with the wrong stuff. Either it was filled with hydrogen and it should have been helium, or vice versa. Whatever it was, they don't do that anymore."

"Thanks for the precise scientific explanation," Hank said, shaking his head. "I think I'll ask my old chemistry professor at the hospital about it. But right now I'm going to fix us a little something to eat while you do your ornaments."

"And why don't you—"

Hank interrupted. He knew what she was going to say. "And why don't I bring us a bottle of Veuve Clicquot. After all, decorating our Christmas tree is worth a bottle of champagne."

"You read my mind," Heaven said without looking around. She'd let the "our Christmas tree" slide. It was, even if she couldn't admit it.

Later, Heaven sat in her robe in the dark watching the tree glow. She'd turned it on again when she remembered the laundry.

Just as she was dozing off, cradled in the curve of Hank's body, she thought of the last load of wash that needed to be put in the dryer. She went down into the kitchen, where the washer and dryer were, turned on the Christmas tree, and changed the load of tights and jeans over to the dryer, then brought the underwear and tee shirts that were dry over to the couch, and folded her clean clothes by Christmas tree light. Because the first floor was one big open space, the whole room sparkled, the lights on the tree reflecting off all the metal surfaces in the kitchen.

Now she sat there clutching the pile of sweet-smelling laundry, burying her nose in it every once in a while. She still used Downy fabric softener, because her mother had. It was a little smell connection that took her through the years. You could smell those Downy clothes and be a protected, loved kid again.

It was like breathing the air someone you loved had breathed in before you, gulping it in as soon as it was exhaled, comforting and sad all at the same time.

Flourless Chocolate Soufflé Cake

12 oz. bittersweet chocolate
12 oz. unsalted butter
12 eggs, separated
1 cup sugar

For years I thought of flourless chocolate cake as a restaurant dessert. Then I realized how easy it was to make at home.

Butter and dust with sugar a nine-inch round cake pan. Preheat oven to 325 degrees. Melt the chocolate and butter in the top of a double boiler or a stainless steel mixing bowl placed over a pan of boiling water. Whisk egg yolks and sugar together until smooth. Whip egg whites into chocolate mixture. Pour both mixtures into prepared pan. Bake 40–45 minutes until cake is cracked on top.

Three

So now I know why all those Santas were running from the blimp disaster yesterday," Heaven said, her voice coming from the interior of a newspaper. The cover photo looked lovely with Heaven's red hair erupting from the top of it, the bright pink blimp draped over the faux Spanish building incongruously, especially when you noticed the six or so Santas in various interpretations of that outfit standing in the foreground of the photo and pointing up at the remains of the blimp.

Sal was already cutting the hair of a businessman who must not have been satisfied with his collar line in the mirror this morning and decided to stop by Sal's for a trim on the way to the office. It was just eight-thirty. Sal looked at Heaven through the mirrors that lined the barber shop and shifted his unlit cigar from one side of his mouth to the other. "I didn't get to the second page yet," he said and jerked his head toward the businessman. Obviously, Sal had been interrupted by this customer before he was finished with the paper. Heaven knew Sal started at the sports section and worked forward.

"The Plaza was having a big Santa contest and the grand prize winner gets a cruise to Alaska next summer." She peeked around the edge of the paper at her audience. "Santa, Alaska, near the North Pole, get it? The judges had just started looking them over when the shooting and stuff happened, so they're going to have the contest again next Sunday. Just one of the fun little sidebars that newspapers find to soften the news of tragedy." Heaven went on to another section.

Sal shook his head. "A blimp crashes into Seville Tower, the pilot's taken out by a sharpshooter, and some slob who doesn't have the sense not to go out of the house in one of those stupid red suits wants to make sure he can still get his damn prize."

Heaven looked up and smiled. "You can even make the feature fluff piece sound dark. That's one of the things I love about you, Sal."

"And of course, I shoulda known when I saw it on the news last night that you were right there in the middle of it. Did Bonnie get the call?" Sal asked.

"Bonnie got the call. They got the body out of there pretty fast, since where he landed wasn't exactly the crime scene and since the whole thing was balling up holiday traffic something fierce," Heaven explained without looking up from the paper. "Bonnie examined the body and told the guy from the coroner's office she'd leave it to him, if anything strange popped up to let her know. He definitely was shot, probably that's what killed him, but you never know. She also sent for the firearms specialist from the evidence team to examine the body and make a few guesses. Bonnie didn't go up on the cherry picker to examine the blimp, said she'd check it out at the warehouse today, said the evidence guys knew better than her what to look for. Of course she didn't really mean that. Bonnie still thinks she's the best at evidence retrieval but I happen to know she's a little afraid of heights."

Sal whisked the neck of his customer with a soft little brush to remove the loose hairs. "I feel sorry for the poor suckers that had to do the door-to-door. Hundreds of shoppers and each one had a different version, I bet."

Heaven chuckled as she folded the paper carefully. Sal didn't like a messy paper in the shop. "It was a real cluster f—I mean, you got that right." Heaven tried not to curse in front of Sal's customers. "Just in the few minutes I stood there with Bonnie, I heard people say that the shots came from all four directions of the compass, I heard that someone had seen a Santa Claus with a compound bow and arrow, someone else was sure the blimp had exploded like a bomb. Bonnie said when you have too many eyewitnesses, you end up with squat." She got up and gave a short salute at the door. "I'm going to work," she announced and left.

As she walked across 39th Street to Café Heaven she felt guilty she hadn't told Sal all the inside news about Foster's chocolate company that she'd obtained from Stephanie Simpson. But somehow she hadn't felt comfortable talking about it in front of Sal's customer. Heaven certainly wouldn't want to start the rumor that her friend Stephanie had bad blood with Foster's Chocolates and had maybe hired a hit man for a blimp. The most innocent remark could turn into vicious gossip in Kansas City. She'd tell Sal later.

• • •

Harold Foster, Jr. sat with his head in his hands. He was a big, handsome man, still with a full crop of wavy, gray hair. His brother, Claude, was pacing in front of Junior's desk. Claude was as tall as his brother, 6' 2" or so, but he had never filled out, didn't have the broad shoulders of a football player like Junior. Now in his sixties, Claude's suits wore him, hanging vacantly over his body. His hair was thin and limp and colorless, and this morning, in his nervousness, he kept pushing it back although nary a strand had crept down to his forehead.

"The insurance team from the company that owns the airship is on the way. I have a car picking them up at the airport and taking them to the police warehouse where the blimp's being examined," Claude said. "Our insurance guys are going to meet with the Plaza this morning. I don't think we hurt their damn building a bit and I told our guys to not take any of that crap about it costing them holiday business. I bet the damn place is packed today with crime scene nuts."

"What about the pilot's family?" Junior asked morosely.

Claude nodded, indicating that that was under control. "He works for the airship people, not us. We're just renting the thing for three months. He had benefits through them. He was driving the Goodyear blimp two months ago; they're like chauffeurs. We don't owe him. I told the guys in Communications to make some calls, find out if he had ten small children or was a Vietnam vet or something else that elicits pity. Also to call the widow and send flowers. You know someone in the press will do a story about the pilot. But I think we're covered."

"I can't believe this happened. Do you think—"

"Junior, don't try to make this more complicated than

it already is," Claude said sharply. "This is just some nut. I think they killed the pilot when all they probably wanted to do was take down a blimp. The world is full of nuts."

Junior drew his body up into a more businesslike position. He had to get a grip and then he had to tell his brother the bad news, not this inexplicable problem of the blimp being shot down. This bad news he, Harold Russell Foster, Jr., had in a sense created. The really bad news. Why had he been so ambitious? He was sixty-seven years old. If he didn't own his own company he'd be retired by now; instead he'd started a big expansion of the business, an addition that was already threatening to destroy everything he'd worked for. "How are we looking for the press conference on Friday?"

Claude Foster grinned. Now they were back on familiar territory. "I've got something in my office to show you," he said and went next door to his own office.

Junior got up and stood by the window, looking out at the workmen running in and out of the newly built addition to the plant, the addition that was the reason for the press conference on Friday.

The company had some corporate offices in downtown Kansas City, but Junior and Claude had always kept their personal offices in the plant. They'd been right here to oversee all this expansion because that's how they liked to do things. Why, Claude had even moved to Texas for three months in 1995 when they had built the plant there. "If you don't pay attention, no one else will," Claude always said.

Claude walked back in with a ten-pound block of chocolate in his hands. It was wrapped in hot pink tin foil and then covered with a paper wrapper with the Foster's logo. "Oh, I know we may tinker with this some more, but we're making up enough of these to give away at the press conference. What do you think?"

Junior Foster, as he had always been called, turned around to see the prototype in his brother's hands, hearing the pride in his brother's voice. "It looks great. I'll be sure to call Janie and tell her they did a good job on the design."

Claude nodded. "They did do a good job, didn't they? I told Janie that this design is to launch our step into second-tier production, that we were going to join elite company."

Junior felt weak, wanted to sit back down, but somehow he thought he had to do this standing up, man to man. "There aren't many folks who process their own cocoa beans and make consumer products. The rest of them are just candy makers."

Claude grinned and put the ten-pound block down on his brother's desk. "This first one is for you. I signed it."

Junior looked down and sure enough, his brother had scrawled, *Another big step for Foster's Chocolates, Love and Thanks, Claude,* and the date, on the top of the package. Junior could feel his breathing become shallow.

"If you hadn't put together the financing for the refining machines, we wouldn't be up there with the big boys," Claude said gratefully.

"Claude, I've made a bad mistake."

"What? What bad mistake? If you think the placement of the—"

Junior cut him off. "Oliver Bodden is coming from Ghana today. He wants to be here for the unveiling of the refining facility."

"Well, that doesn't sound so bad. The second-stage

production man from West Africa who helped finance this, sure he'd want to come."

"Oliver is insisting that we use only West African nibs, that we can't blend. He says they'll pull out if we don't do it their way, says we still need more of their money for the distribution and all the new inventory."

Claude shook his head vehemently. "What are you talking about? Every second-tier producer blends nibs from all over the world. That's what makes a company's chocolate have an individual taste. No one just uses cocoa from one place. That would be suicide."

"I told him that. I asked why they would want to see us fail, that it was in their interests for us to have a product that would compete with all the Swiss and Belgian second-tier producers. He said . . . ," Junior paused, fighting for air. He thought he might just fall into a faint right then and there. "He said that would be a pity, now wouldn't it, and they'd have to take over the company if we went under, that they were our largest lender.

"He said we had signed a contract for him to provide some experienced production managers, to help train our people. They would report back to him and make sure we weren't trying to sneak in any nibs from other countries."

"Oh, I get it," Claude said angrily. "He brings a bunch of spies in here to watch us, and when we go broke because of this exclusivity thing, he and his partners take over and they can use a sensible blend of nibs and make a killing. That'll happen over their dead bodies!"

Junior smiled wanly. "I think the phrase is, over *my* dead body."

Claude wasn't in the mood to be corrected. "They plan to make money off our failure. But you're right, it will have to be over someone else's dead body, because no one is going to run us out of business so easily. Did you check the contracts? Do we have to do what he says?"

Junior shrugged. "It states that decisions about second-tier production, when there's a dispute, will be the authority of the West African Cacao Company, as they are the experts at refining, etc., etc. I've got the legal department going over it with a fine-toothed comb now."

Claude pushed at his thinning hair and almost shrieked at his brother. "Now! Oh, great. Now's the time to have legal on overtime, after the horse is out of the barn."

"I doubt anyone in legal would have thought before this that a company would invest millions and then sabotage the product they'd invested in," Junior pointed out. "Besides, it sounded good on paper, to have the folks who've already been doing that kind of work be here to guide us. Normally, you would take their advice."

"So now, for the five million they threw in for this second-stage facility, they might be able to pick up a third-stage operation worth half a billion, that is, if they put us out of business. What a bargain," Claude hissed. "Well, we're just not going to let that happen. We're going to make the best damn chocolate, no matter what it takes. We've been ruthless before. These guys don't know who they're dealing with."

Junior looked back out the window at the back of the plant. "Yeah, we're two wheeler-dealers in Kansas City who gypped the rest of our family out of millions of dollars. Watch out, world," he said quietly.

"I know you've ordered beans from Brazil and Mexico and I don't want you to cancel those orders. They won't get away with this." Claude grabbed the gift block of chocolate off his brother's desk and walked out.

Junior stared into space a few minutes longer, then walked over to the phone and dialed. "Janie, its Junior."

"Hi, Uncle. What can I do for you?" The voice on the other end was businesslike.

"I just wanted to tell you, Claude showed me the package for the ten-pound blocks and you did a great job. It looks very nice."

"Boy, Uncle, you really know how to throw around a compliment. 'It looks very nice,' well, whoopee." The voice had warmed up slightly, had a little tease in it.

Junior smiled. "That was a Midwestern compliment, Janie. I don't want to spoil you. It looks terrific. You're a good graphic designer."

"Thanks, boss."

"Janie, I would like you to come to this press conference we're having down here at the plant on Friday," Junior said, and hesitated, looking for the right words. "It would mean a lot to me to have you there, you know . . ."

"You mean as the only member of the rest of the Foster family that will speak to you?" The voice was laughing now.

"Will you come?" Junior tried not to ever talk about the family breach.

"Hey, I'm as curious as the next guy. Even though I've been working on the designs, I don't really know what's going down. So, Uncle, I'll be there with bells on. Oh, by the way, sorry about the blimp, another thing I didn't know about."

"You know the marketing guys, always coming up with something. This time it didn't work out very well. I'll see you Friday then," Junior said, hanging up the phone absently. His mind was already on to the next thing: how to save his company.

Marie Whitmer hadn't really meant to listen in. Usually when the brothers were meeting together they didn't even bother to close the door. It wasn't completely closed this time. But Marie couldn't help but notice when Junior came in that he was preoccupied, seemed worried today. Then when he'd told her about the fellow coming from Africa and others following him and to get them all hotel rooms, she could tell something wasn't right. She'd worked for the brothers for twenty years. She knew them like the back of her hand. Yes, something was wrong. Proof of that was how Claude had just stormed out of Junior's office, slamming the door of his own office shut. He never did that. He liked to be able to call to Marie instead of using the intercom.

Marie, feeling uneasy about what she was about to do, did it anyway. She picked up the phone and dialed, swiveling her chair to turn her body away from the brothers' offices.

Sitting at the bar at the Fairmont Hotel, looking out at the Plaza, Oliver Bodden had to concede Kansas City was lovely. The lights on all the buildings were a nice touch. He looked down at the newspaper beside his martini glass, and smiled again at the photograph of the ruined blimp. Foster's was already in trouble. The brothers might try to make light of this tragedy, but it wasn't good.

"Quite a story, eh?" The woman sitting two barstools down gave him a smile and indicated the newspaper.

"Well, yes, it looks as if I've arrived in town one day too late for the excitement," Oliver said in that lovely, clipped British accent of his. "Are you staying here at the hotel and did you happen to see anything?" he asked politely.

"Oh, no," she said. "I'm not a guest. I live here in town. I like to stop here on my way home from work for a drink, especially at Christmastime. It's the best view of the Plaza."

"And did it happen right over there, then?" Oliver indicated the shopping center out the window.

In twenty minutes the woman was sitting next to Oliver sipping a fresh glass of white wine, the Kistler Chardonnay. She had given him an amusing rendition of the demise of the blimp; it seemed she'd been doing some Christmas shopping on the Plaza at the time.

He looked sideways at her now. She was attractive enough and he did have the evening to kill.

"Can I tell you something without embarrassing you?" she asked suddenly and quite provocatively.

"Oh, dear, I hope so," Oliver said with a smile.

"I love your skin. It's so black its almost blue."

Oliver assessed the woman again. "Well, I was born and still live in West Africa. My ancestors had the advantage over your American blacks of not having to have sex with the master, now didn't they? Or if they did, slavery being a rather ugly part of Africa's past as well, the master was as black as they, so we haven't had much in the way of dilution. Thank you for the compliment, though. Would you like to have dinner with me? My business associates won't be here for another day so I find myself without a dining companion."

. . .

Heaven went out into the dining room of Café Heaven and proclaimed to anyone who would listen, "I'm whipped. You all beat me up tonight." She'd worked the saute station and now she headed for the bar. "Tony, dear, get me a glass of the Mount Veeder Cab, will you please, and Sara is going to give you the bits and pieces of what was left of the short ribs on some mashed potatoes for me. I'm starved."

Chris Snyder and Joe Long, the two waiters who were also the producers of the Monday night open mike program came up and sat down by Heaven, one on each side. "What a great night. The place was packed," Chris said as he worked on his check-out sheet.

"How'd you like the blimp piece?" Joe asked proudly. Joe and Chris, well known for their performance art pieces, had found some bright pink plastic plus wire from the hardware store and somehow made an outfit out of it that resembled a blimp only loosely. They walked out into the dining room in it with just their legs showing. The contraption was hooked up to a bicycle tire pump and the big pink thing then exploded, spraying a shower of Foster's candy that the boys tossed throughout the crowd.

Heaven smiled and waited until her mouth was empty to answer. "In terrible taste but pretty damn funny, I must admit. I peeked at you guys from the pass-through."

"I think the real blimp should have been filled with candy like ours was. It would have been a much better advertisement," Chris said.

"Maybe the city wouldn't let them drop objects from the blimp. Someone could get their eye put out with a peanut cluster," Heaven said.

Joe turned around. "Oh, look, here comes 'the city' now."

It was Sergeant Bonnie Weber coming in the door of the café. She walked up to the bar and Joe got out of his seat and bowed low to her. "Please, Detective, sit here. I'm on my way home. Heaven, don't forget you promised to go with me to the women's body building contest Wednesday night."

Heaven looked up from her plate. "How could I forget? I've been looking forward to it for weeks. 'Night, guys." The two young men went toward the office to check out.

Bonnie looked at her quizzically. "You have? Been looking forward to a body building contest, I mean?"

"Well, I've never been to one so it should be fun. A friend of Joe's is competing and he wants to support her. What's up with you, out so late? Are you off duty yet? Can you have a beverage of your choice?"

Bonnie shook her head. "Too many questions. Yes, I'm done. I had to go give a speech at the Westport Library, how to save life and limb in this busy mugging season. And I would love a Boulevard beer, please, Tony."

Heaven hadn't really given her friend enough shit about passing her sergeants exam, which she'd done earlier in the year. "Now that you're in the big time, Sergeant, you get the big-time cases, like the blimp sniper. You get to go give speeches. You're a BFD."

Bonnie smiled. "Everything but the big-effing-deal salary." She looked around. "It's nice to come here without having a dead body to deal with."

"Oh, now, you come for social reasons sometimes. You and the family were in here just last month," Heaven reminded her. "Why don't I get the feeling this is just a social occasion?"

"Because you're a cynical, with-it, new century gal, a gal who isn't easily fooled, but a gal who will always do a favor for a friend."

"Oh, brother. What is it?"

"Well, I seem to recall from our conversation on Sunday you're going down to the Chocolate Queen tomorrow."

"And?"

"By the way, I love the way Stephanie took your Barbecue Queen name and used it for the chocolate shop."

"Yes, that way those that know her as a Barbecue Queen will already want to come to buy her chocolates," Heaven said impatiently. "But I doubt you want me to talk marketing strategy with Stephanie. What *do* you want me to talk about?"

"Oh, you know, just try to get a little more information about this Foster family rift. I asked her again after you left on Sunday but she seemed spooked, not that what happened wasn't enough to spook a person. I just thought that maybe someone on her side of the family had threatened to get even with those who had control of the hen who lays those golden eggs, or chocolate eggs in this case. They must sell millions of them at Easter."

Heaven shook her head and pushed back her plate. "Tony, I think there's one piece of flourless chocolate torte left back in the kitchen. Will you find it for me, please? And two forks."

Bonnie's eyebrows raised.

Heaven shrugged. "Beer and chocolate is a perfectly legit combination. So Bonnie, you want me to get my friend to confide some horrible family secret so I can rat it out to you?"

"Don't be so dramatic. I need help here. I did a background check on the pilot and he led an extremely normal life. No big debt. No angry ex-wives. No known enemies. So I have to concentrate on the company angle and I just thought that if you were going to learn about chocolate, whatever that means, you could be the lovable but nosy person you usually are."

"Well, I am curious, of course," Heaven said, rather innocently. "I'd already planned to try to find out more about how the chocolate business works. I guess that could include a few questions about Foster's. But if she confesses to something horrible, not that I think she will, I'm not sure what my moral obligation will be."

Bonnie huffed and made a *puhtttttt* sound. "Stephanie was sitting with you when the sniper fired. I doubt that she could have taken down that blimp and killed the pilot by remote control. In other words, I'm not expecting some tearful confession of guilt that you'll then have to feel guilty about telling me. Although she acted strange on Sunday. Do you think your friend Stephanie could have hired a hit man to avenge her mother's honor?"

"I am absolutely certain she wouldn't do that. On the other hand, I've been wrong before, as we both know. A week doesn't go by that someone who hasn't recovered from a divorce kills another someone, although it's usually men who react that way. Jesus, Bonnie, don't make me discover my good buddy Stephanie has gone over to the dark side."

Bonnie wasn't going to go there. "Stop being so dramatic. Just ask the kind of snoopy questions you'd ask anyway, okay? You'll be aware if there's anything I should know."

Heaven turned and threw her arm around her friend's shoulder. "Are you saying you trust my judgment?"

Bonnie signaled the bartender for another beer. "I wouldn't go that far," she said with a little grin.

Choc-O-Rama Brownies

8 oz. semisweet baking chocolate
2 sticks butter (1 cup)
¾ cup cocoa
2 cups brown sugar
1 egg
1 tsp. vanilla
1 ¼ cups flour
¼ tsp. salt

Preheat oven to 350 degrees. Grease an 8- or 9-inch baking pan. In a double boiler or bain marie, melt the baking chocolate. In another saucepan, melt the butter. Combine cocoa and brown sugar, and stir in the melted butter. Beat in egg and vanilla.

Add the melted chocolate. Stir in the flour and salt and beat until smooth. Pour mixture into the pan and bake for 45 minutes or until brownies begin to pull away from the sides of the pan. Cool before cutting. Thanks to my friend and fellow food writer, Charles Ferruza, for the recipe.

Four

"Try to pay attention and don't ask too many questions until the end," Stephanie said.

"About what we're doing or about chocolate in general?" Heaven asked as she stirred some chocolate that was melting in the top of a double boiler set on a Bunsen burner–like affair.

"Didn't you just ask me to give you a brief history of chocolate?" Stephanie snapped, like a third-grade schoolteacher reprimanding a child who wasn't sitting still.

Heaven's eyes widened. "Yes, Mrs. Simpson."

"Okay, then. Don't hold me to any of this exactly. I had no idea that people would want me to come to their schools and gourmet groups and talk about chocolate but they do. So I've had to study up, although I know what they really want are the free samples at the end of the talk."

"Enough with the disclaimers. I'm not going to go over to Foster's Chocolates and tell them Stephanie said you put wax in your chocolates. This is just for me. So, I do have enough sense to know chocolate came from the New World, as they call us over here. Mexico?"

"That's where the European adventurers found it. And who said anything about stupid old Foster's? I don't mention them in my speeches, just for spite. But back to Mexico. There's a great reference to that in one of my chocolate books. It's from a letter written by one of Cortez's soldiers. He said the Aztec emperor Montezuma drank fifty cups of chocolate a day out of golden goblets, said it was an aphrodisiac."

"Something I've never really understood," Heaven admitted.

Stephanie looked over slyly. "Maybe you just haven't had the right combination of chocolate and—"

Heaven cut in hurriedly. "Let's keep on with the history lesson. Montezuma drank a lot of chocolate. The evil white guy plunderers from Europe took it back home with them. Then what?"

"I should mention that it probably originated in South America, just like the tomato. But they both got 'discovered' when they were cultivated in Mexico. The Indians of Mexico were obviously very evolved, cuisinewise. Chocolate was used by both the Olmecs and the Mayans before the Aztecs. But the names 'chocolate' and 'cocoa' are both derived from Aztec. 'Cocoa' meant the tree it grew on and 'chocolate' meant bitter water. And it sure would be, bitter I mean, if you drank the stuff straight like Montezuma did."

"I think my chocolate is melted," Heaven said, looking down at her bowl.

"Throw in that piece of butter beside you and keep stirring," Stephanie instructed. "So for the first hundred years or so, chocolate was just a drink in Europe, no baked goods, no candy. They added stuff to it, ground nuts and sugar and cinnamon, to flavor the drink, but no one made candy with it until they learned how to process it better."

"And when did that happen?" Heaven asked, wondering when she could steer the conversation to Foster's again. She'd been shut down in her first attempt.

"Eighteen twenty-eight," Stephanie said, proud of knowing the exact year.

Shit, we've got one hundred and seventy something years to go, Heaven thought. "What happened in 1828?"

"Cocoa beans are more than half cocoa butter, did you know that?" Stephanie was warming to her subject. "In 1828, a Dutch man named Conrad Van Houten invented a screw press that removed most of the butter from the bean. You ended up with cocoa powder and cocoa butter."

"So that's why we call it Dutch chocolate?"

"Not really," Stephanie said dismissively. She wasn't going to be hurried. "Then you added some of the cocoa butter back in to the cocoa powder, along with sugar, and it's much smoother, it's 'eating' chocolate. It became all the rage. Did you know that in World War Two, soldiers would sometimes get just three bars of chocolate to last them a whole day in battle?"

"Boy, a bunch of troops seriously jazzed up on chocolate. No wonder we won. I remember the time Iris, she couldn't have been more than eight, ate three Hershey's with almonds. She didn't come down for days."

"Now, do you want to know how cocoa beans get to be these blocks of chocolate we have here?" Stephanie asked sweetly. She was pouring melted milk chocolate into big metal Santa Claus molds.

"You bet I do," Heaven said. This would at least lead to Foster's eventually. It had to.

"Well, first the cocoa pods are harvested and broken apart and the pulp and the beans set out in the sun where they ferment. Things happen," Stephanie said as she left the molded Santas to set up and deftly tossed some popcorn in a large copper bowl of dark melted chocolate. She threw in some toasted macadamia nuts that had been broken up.

"Things happen? That's sounds like me trying to describe blimps to Hank. What happens?"

Stephanie gave Heaven a superior smile. "It gets hot and it kills the seeds' embryos, for one thing. The cell walls are broken down and the astringent phenolic compounds bind together. So there."

"I'm assuming this is all good news," Heaven tried gallantly. She really did want to know about chocolate but at this rate it would be News Year's Eve before she got out of here.

"Yes, it is. Now the beans are cleaned up and dried out and shipped to second-tier producers."

"Up till now, it's been first tier?"

"That's right," Stephanie said with a little surprise in her voice. Heaven was obviously interested and paying attention. "The second tier is the chocolate factory where—"

"Like Foster's?" Heaven interrupted.

Stephanie shook her head. "No, no. Foster's is a candymaker. That's third tier. Now listen."

"I know, and don't interrupt you or you'll start all over at the Aztecs," Heaven said with a laugh. She could see there was no quick way to do this.

"The beans come into the chocolate factory. The chocolate factories are mostly in Switzerland, Belgium, and England. Callebaut and Valrhona are two kinds I use," Stephanie said, pointing to two big blocks of chocolate sitting on the counter, "and they're two of the best and most expensive."

"You would." Heaven too, always used the best ingredients she could afford and it didn't surprise her that Stephanie did the same.

"So first, the beans are roasted, then a winnowing machine cracks open the seeds. There are these little morsels inside the shells and they are called nibs. Now this is where a chocolate factory gets its distinctive style."

"From the nibs?" Heaven asked, deciding to just be a good student for a while and not try to lead the conversation.

"From blending nibs from all over the world and from different estates from the same country, just like a winemaker would."

"Who grows most of the cocoa?"

"It's called cacao until it's broken down to the seeds, then it's cocoa."

"Sorry," Heaven said quickly. "Who grows most of the cacao?"

"West Africa and Brazil. Any place within twenty degrees north or south of the equator can grow cacao trees though. So the chocolate manufacturer blends their nibs, then the nibs are ground under heat. The stuff is then called chocolate liquor."

"Is it alcoholic?"

"No, and don't ask me why its called liquor, it just is," Stephanie said as she went over to the sink and washed some chocolaty popcorn chunks off her hands. "The next step is a big one," she said dramatically. Even she was getting a little impatient. "This is where they put the chocolate liquor under hydraulic pressure and extract the cocoa butter. The other part that's not cocoa butter is called cocoa solids. Drizzle that ganache on these, Jackson Pollack style." She pushed a baking sheet of brownies Heaven's way. They already had a sheen of milk chocolate frosting on top.

"I've got it, liquor becomes butter and solids," Heaven recited as she drizzled her dark chocolate ganache over the tops of the brownies.

"But the chocolate would still have a gritty feel to it, if you tasted it at this stage. You have to refine it, which is where these big steel rollers grind the particles real small. Then it's conched."

Heaven knew if she didn't bite, Stephanie would be disappointed. "Conch, like the sea animal they make fritters out of?"

"Rodolphe Lindt—Lindt still makes chocolate—invented this machine that was shaped like conch shells. It smoothes the chocolate in these troughs, back and forth, back and forth. I saw them when I went to Switzerland."

"Oh, so you took part of your divorce settlement and went on a chocolate tour," Heaven said teasingly.

"I had to know about this stuff, didn't I? Now listen, we're almost done. The conching also evaporates the acids and makes the chocolate smoother. And it's done under heat. Everything's done under heat. Now the chocolate has to be tempered. It has to be cooled down then heated back up again. Hot, cool, hot. That stabilizes the cocoa butter crystals that are left in the chocolate so they won't turn the chocolate grainy again."

"Whew, are we done yet?"

"Yes," Stephanie said solemnly. "Then it's put in these ten-pound blocks and away it goes, to candymakers. That's an industry term for anyone who does the third-tier work, producing actual chocolate confections. Everyone from Godiva to me is a candymaker."

Now, Heaven thought. Surely now. "And this is where Foster's fits in to the picture?"

"Yes, even someone as big as Foster's doesn't do their own second-tier production. I think only Hershey's in America does both, oh, and also someone around San Francisco, and maybe one someone else."

"Steph, when you were growing up, did you ever talk about Foster's, or was it a forbidden subject?"

Stephanie was scooping chocolate popcorn into clear bags, weighing them as she filled them. "You know, it wasn't like that. It wasn't forbidden but we didn't talk about it either. Sometimes when we'd be at a holiday celebration, Mom or Aunt Carol would say, 'I wonder what they're doing over on the other side of the tracks,' some crack like that. But it always made my grandmother uncomfortable and so we didn't tease about the brothers if she was around. We didn't eat Foster's chocolates either."

"I had one more question I was going to ask you on Sunday, before we were so rudely interrupted. How's the company doing? Do you ever hear anything about it from your grandmother?"

"Why do you ask?" Stephanie replied with a definite chill in her voice.

"Oh, they asked me to be at this press conference on Friday and I just wondered what it was about. I know they're going to talk about the New Year's Eve thing but the person who called me last week, you know, some PR girl, said they had a big announcement to make. I just thought you might know."

Stephanie started cleaning up her work area, wiping everything down with bleach water the same way Heaven did at the restaurant. "I'm sure I wouldn't know. The only person on the poor side of the family who has anything to do with Junior and Claude is my cousin Jane."

"Is that Junior's daughter or something?" Heaven asked, then remembered Stephanie had specified the poor side of the family. It couldn't be Junior's daughter.

"No, Junior has two daughters and Claude has a boy. None of them live in Kansas City or work for the company elsewhere. Jane is my Aunt Carol's only child."

Uh, oh. A traitor. "So Jane speaks to her uncles. How come?"

"It's worse than that. Jane actually works for Foster's. She's in charge of the graphic design department. It really upset Mom and Aunt Carol. But Jane, we call her Janie, has always been a bit of a problem."

"How a problem?" Heaven asked.

"When she was a kid, she was fat. Then she had bulimia or something. I remember Mom and Dad talking about it, Mom telling Dad how he was a doctor and he had to help. Janie got as thin as a rail when we were in high school."

"And now? Oh, do you see her or is she banished because of her job?"

"Oh, no. My mother would never do that. I see her three or four times a year. Now she's a health nut, with an emphasis on the 'nut.' She brings enough vitamins to a family dinner to choke a horse. And she has to take them in just the right order, some before, some after she eats."

Heaven had lost interest in cousin Jane. She didn't think she'd learned much for Bonnie Weber. "At least she doesn't sneak in your bathroom and puke. Now can we talk about my masterpiece?"

"What do you want to make?"

Heaven shrugged. "I want it to have at least three different treatments of chocolate, but I don't know if it's a cake or ice cream or what. I want something about it to be surrealistic, like art."

"Well, the body part thing has been done. Even here on the Plaza I sell chocolate legs and breasts. I can't do a chocolate penis or I'd lose my lease. So you don't want to do body parts."

"What about animals?" Heaven asked.

"No, too easy. Think chocolate Easter rabbit. I'll think about it overnight but I do know one thing it has to have," Stephanie said.

"What's that?"

"You're a chef. Whatever it is, it has to have a big chocolate cleaver sticking out of it."

Joe Long and Heaven Lee walked into the Woodside Racquet Club. An easel in the lobby told them the semifinals of the women's body building contest was across the street in the gym. Woodside was a health club, swimming pool and tennis court complex just to the west of the Plaza. Heaven and Joe headed across the street, walking fast to keep out of the cold. The sunny, forty-degree days turned into nippy, twenty-degree nights as soon as the sun went down.

"I smell snow," Joe said happily.

"Me too," Heaven agreed. "I can hardly wait. We haven't had a good snow yet. There was that little, half-ass snow shower around Thanksgiving."

The gym was steamy with bodies and the air smelled of sweat socks, expensive aftershave and disinfectant. Even upper-middle-class bodies perspired. The aerobics classes at peak times were held in the gym, along with step, yoga and Tae Bo. There were also men's and women's basketball teams sponsored by the club. But tonight, the bleachers had been pulled down and a stage had been erected under one basketball hoop. It had the energy of a small-town beauty contest or talent show. Heaven and Joe looked around.

"I wonder if it's like a wedding," Joe murmured. "I'd hate to sit on the wrong side."

The crowd seemed to be equally divided on the two sides of the gym, sitting about halfway up on each side. "Where's your friend?" Heaven asked.

"Oh, I'm sure they're all in the back, oiling up their bodies. I wouldn't want to bother her. They get nervous, just like us actors," Joe said with authority. "Let's sit down."

It was then that Heaven noticed the Foster's Chocolate banner, hanging above the door they had just come in. "Foster's Chocolate, the Athlete's Friend," the banner proclaimed. "Boy, every place you look, there's Foster's," she said.

Joe went right over to a big fishbowl of various Foster's Chocolate bars that was on a table by the doors leading in and out of the gym. "Well, it is their fiftieth anniversary. This is a pretty slick tie-in, because body builders are secret chocolate junkies. Kathy told me that." He grabbed several wrapped confections. "I love the cashew and caramel turtles."

Heaven poked around and came up with a green foil package. "I like these, the Mint Dreams. Mint stuff like marshmallow fluff covered with milk chocolate. Really disgusting and wonderful."

Heaven and Joe started toward the bleachers, stuffing their candy in their coat pockets. But they didn't get very far.

Loud voices were the first clue something was going on. They were coming from the locker room area, but soon the doors to that area opened up and the yelling, along with the people doing the yelling, spilled out onto the gym floor. The crowd, having come for a show, perked up, heads turned toward the noise like they were at a tennis match.

"Uh-oh. It's my friend Kathy. Come on," Joe said and started across the gym.

Someone from the club started following him. "You can't wear those shoes on the gym floor," they shouted. Joe had on some Prada boots with thick soles. He paid no attention to the admonition, making a beeline for the trouble. Heaven, however, took the route around the playing floor and still got there in time to get the drift of what was going on.

"I know you're behind this, you bitch," a women Heaven assumed to be Joe's friend was yelling. She assumed this because Joe had grabbed hold of the woman's arm. "This is a ridiculous allegation. I'm the mother of two, for God's sake."

Kathy, if Heaven was correct about it being Kathy, was a masculine-looking woman. Probably in her mid-forties, she did not have a pretty face; it was worn and leathery from too much sun. Still, she was attractive, very neat, very buffed, blond hair cut short, arms bulging beneath her T-shirt. It was impossible to tell if she had nice eyes because right now they were black and glittering with anger. The woman she was yelling at was in a robe, her hardened body gleaming with oil that would now have to be replaced. She too, had short blond hair, but was slightly younger, shorter and slimmer than Joe's friend.

"I guess the doctors will tell us if that's possible," the younger woman said with a sneer.

Another woman, fully dressed and with a worried look on her face and a clipboard in her hand, stepped between the two contestants. "Let's be calm, here. Kathy, this will not keep you out of the finals on Sunday. You have enough points already. Just keep the appointment tomorrow and everything will be fine."

"Oh, don't worry, I'm going to your fucking appointment. But this is not over. Not by a long shot. You're all a bunch of jealous, backbiting—"

"Kathy, come with us," Joe said quickly and took his friend by the arm, turning her around and starting toward the door.

Heaven lagged behind Joe and Kathy. She watched the official and the alleged troublemaker put their heads together. The clipboard lady was attempting to calm the younger contestant, who seemed near tears. Then, as the clipboard woman walked away, the younger woman did a curious thing, at least Heaven thought it was curious. She took a Mint Dream—Heaven would have recognized that green foil from fifty yards away— out of her robe pocket, unwrapped it and started eating it, looking around to see if anyone was watching her. Even under the threat of being seen eating a Mint Dream at a body building exhibition, the solace of chocolate was just too strong. Heaven wondered if men secretly ate Snickers bars when they were upset.

Heaven caught up with Joe and Kathy just as they'd retrieved Kathy's coat from the locker room. "I told Kathy we'd just go over to the café and have a drink," Joe said, looking at Heaven for support.

"Kathy, I'm Heaven Lee. What happened back there?"

Kathy stuck her hand out to shake Heaven's. "Kathy

Hager, glad to meet you. Sorry about all this. It was nice of you to come with my buddy here." She punched Joe's arm like a jock, then turned back toward Heaven. "Someone, and I know it was that bitch back there, put in a protest questioning my gender. I have to go tomorrow and prove I'm not a man."

Heaven was momentarily speechless. She had a terrible impulse to laugh. She repressed this inappropriate reaction and offered what she could. "You're right, Joe. A drink on me at the café. We're only a few blocks away. Why don't you ride with your friend and I'll go back by myself."

In just a few minutes, Heaven, Joe and Kathy Hager were sitting at the bar, clinking their glasses full of Herradura margaritas together. "To Kathy, who will be the body building champ of Kansas City on Sunday," Joe said, trying hard to lift the pall off the evening.

"The woman body building champ," Kathy said tersely.

"Kathy, does this happen often, that someone's gender would come into doubt?" Heaven asked. "I know nothing about your sport, so I'm sorry if that's a stupid question."

Kathy shook her head. "The only time I can remember hearing about a gender protest was in '99 in England. It was a runner, I think. I remember she was a mother, too."

"What will they do?" Joe asked.

"At the doc's?" Kathy replied. "A blood test and a physical exam. It's just fuckin' embarrassing, is what it is. This town is full of egomaniacs."

Heaven assumed Kathy was a butch lesbian but maybe she wasn't. Not every masculine woman was, and Kathy had just mentioned her children. Heaven felt slightly ashamed that she had gone for an easy categorization. "How long have you been body building?"

"At least ten years. My partner, I had the same relationship for twenty years, was in the sport and she got me interested."

Joe quickly broke in. "Heaven, Kathy's partner died of breast cancer last year."

"I'm sorry." Heaven decided she could ask about the kids now, since Kathy was willing to talk personally. "What about your kids? Were you married to a man or did you adopt with your partner?"

"No, I was married to Gene Hager for eight years and both the girls are his, both born before I turned twenty. We lived back East, in Philadelphia. My girls loved Courtney though. They have been real good about my change of lifestyle."

"How did you get from Philadelphia to Kansas City?"

"Jobs. Now I teach at UMKC. American history. Courtney"—Kathy had trouble saying her name and gulped—"worked in the business world," she said vaguely.

Heaven didn't want to ask any more painful questions about this woman's dead lover. Kathy had had enough grief tonight, accused of trying to sneak in a body building contest she wasn't equipped for. Heaven was thinking about how hard it would be to tell Iris something like Kathy had told her daughters. *Hi, girls, I'm a lesbian now.* She wondered what the daughters' sexualities were; Kathy must have read her thoughts.

"Both of my daughters are wonderful and supportive. They're both married to men—one lives in Baltimore, and one in Omaha. I've got three grandkids," she said proudly.

Heaven thought of her own five marriages. "It's amazing how much our kids will accept from us, isn't it? I've been married five times and have one daughter. She just went on loving me, no matter what stupid stuff I did."

"So, what happens at these body building contests?" Joe asked, trying to avoid anymore maudlin mothers' confessional between the two women.

Kathy was willing to explain. "Well, the judges award points for arms, back, leg and thigh together, calves, hamstrings, traps, overall body and best poser. You can win several of the categories and still not get best overall. And the crowds are very fickle. They get behind someone almost every season and when you have the crowd, it really helps you pose better."

Heaven hadn't seen enough to tell if Kathy had the crowd this season or not. She didn't have to wait long to know.

"This year, little miss nosy bitch Jane is their favorite. I can't figure it. She's so serious, she comes off angry on stage. I don't find that attractive at all."

Joe and Heaven were at a loss as to how to make Kathy feel better. Heaven signaled the bartender. "One more for the road, Tony."

"Oh look, it's snowing," Joe said, clapping his hands with glee.

The windows in the front of the restaurant revealed lots of wet snowflakes coming down like crazy. "I have to go look. I love 39th Street when it snows," Heaven said and went toward the front door. "You guys visit. Kathy, I know this will all turn out all right. Go to that doctor and show 'em your stuff."

Thirty-ninth Street was right in the middle of Kansas City, about halfway between downtown and the Plaza. It was a part of town generally left to the marketplace to decide its fortune, never receiving big government handouts for rehab. The storefronts were always rented, some to trendy businesses, some to old-fashioned businesses like Sal's and the hardware store and the tattoo parlor. A faction of the newer store owners would rather not have had a tattoo parlor in their midst. Heaven didn't mind it. She liked it that 39th Street was driven by what people wanted and needed in their lives, not by some fancy developer's ideas of what people wanted.

The big medical center six blocks away dictated that the neighborhood had affordable housing, cafés and bars and things like a Laundromat and a dry cleaners for the med students, and also florists for people to frequent before they visited their sick relatives.

Sal's Barbershop was a fixture. Heaven couldn't imagine 39th Street without Sal's.

Quite a few contemporary restaurants, like Café Heaven, had sprung up on 39th Street, the rents still making it affordable to open there if you weren't a national chain.

Right now, at ten at night, even though several businesses, including Café Heaven, were open and full of people, the street was silent in that way that snow can make a cityscape silent.

No cars had muddied the snow-covered pavement with tire marks yet.

Everything sparkled.

Absorbing the hustle and bustle of the day, camouflaging the mundane ugliness of chipped paint and graffiti and dog poop, the snowflakes had transformed a Plain Jane street into Cinderella.

Heaven slipped out the front door of the restaurant and danced down the middle of 39th Street for a minute, all by herself, making big figure eights in the fresh snow in her Italian high-heeled boots.

Nutella Chocolate Chip Cookies

½ cup butter, unsalted (1 stick)
½ cup brown sugar
½ cup Nutella, the chocolate/hazelnut spread
2 large eggs
1 vanilla bean, split lengthwise, pulp scraped out
2 ⅓ cups flour
1 tsp. baking soda
1 tsp. salt
12 oz. bittersweet chocolate, chopped into small pieces
½ cup chopped hazelnuts, if desired

Heat oven to 375 degrees.

With an electric mixer, or by hand if you're macho, cream the butter and sugar. Add the Nutella. Beat in the eggs and the vanilla pulp until well mixed.

In another bowl, sift together the flour, baking soda and salt. Gradually add the dry ingredients to the butter mixture. Mix in the chocolate and nuts. The mixture is crumbly, but remember, you have lots of chocolate to bind it together in the baking process. Drop spoonfuls of dough on a baking sheet lined with parchment paper or sprayed with baking spray. Flatten the dough and bake until lightly browned, 9–12 minutes. Cool before removing the cookies from the baking sheet.

Five

Oliver Bodden sat in Junior Foster's office, nonchalantly reading the paper. Junior walked in, his hands full of papers, and glowered when he saw Oliver. "You still here?" Junior said tersely.

"I think you and Claude are right to have your offices down here at the plant," Oliver said, ignoring the other man's rudeness. "I took a look around and I think I found a space that will be a perfect little nook for me."

Junior snorted. "That's what the operations foreman tells me. Said you told him to start drawing up some plans. Since when is a thousand square feet considered a little nook?"

Oliver folded the paper carefully and looked around the room. "I would think any amount of space would be fine with you, just to get me out of your own rather spacious office."

"Funny you never mentioned needing an office before this," Junior said as he made piles on his desk of photocopies and file folders. " 'Course there were lots of things you didn't mention." He suddenly slumped down into his chair, sitting hard, forlorn with the realization of what a mess he'd made.

Oliver smiled at the other man's pain. Foolish fellow to take this all so personally. He stood up and buttoned his suit jacket, today a Saville Row navy worsted with a tiny red stripe, and automatically straightened his tie, red with a small blue pattern. "Are you ready for the big press conference tomorrow?"

Junior Foster nodded. "Oh, it'll be a good show. The mayor is coming, along with several members of the city council and some of the chefs who will be making chocolate creations for our big charity extravaganza on New Year's Eve." His voice was flat and lifeless.

Claude walked in. If it was possible, he had shrunk in the last few days, his suit looking even more like it was walking around without him, his hair thinner and more colorless. He reeked of miserable. He shot a hard look at his brother, then turned to Oliver. "There was a message on my desk to be here at six for a meeting. What's that about?"

Junior looked blank and shrugged his shoulders.

Oliver checked his watch and went over to the windows that overlooked the new addition to the plant. The plant was only running one shift, the Christmas candy rush over a month ago and the candy shipped. The place was deserted, silent, the area outside the building spotless in anticipation of the visitors the next day. "And here you are, Claude, right on time. I like working with people who follow directions." Oliver gestured for the two men to join him. "Your brother and I were just talking about how tomorrow was going to be quite a show. Well, I have a little show for the two of you right now."

Junior and Claude walked cautiously toward the windows. "What in the hell are you talking about?" Claude snapped. He made no pretense of civility to Oliver Bodden since Junior had confessed the snags in their agreement. The man was a snake, and no better than a common thug who snatches other people's property on the street. The sooner the lawyers figured out how to get West African Cacao out of this partnership, the better.

As the three men peered down at the concrete pad between the old part of the factory and the new part, a parade of six forklifts came around the corner, each manned by one of the "advisors" from Africa, men who had arrived in Kansas City earlier that day. The forklifts were piled with burlap sacks of cocoa beans.

Oliver turned to the brothers with an ugly smile on his face, the smile a combination of triumph and anticipation of what was going to happen next. "Unfortunately you didn't follow my most important direction, when I told you that Foster's would be using only nibs from my country, and my company." The forklifts were dumping the sacks of beans in a big pile in the middle of the concrete pad. "When I was searching for a space to locate my office, look what I found. Buried under beans from my country were beans from Brazil, from Mexico, even from the island of Samoa, a locale that I didn't know grew cacao trees. Very enterprising of you to locate them. Too bad you won't be able to use them."

Two of the men who worked for Oliver down on the pad were now splashing gasoline from red cans over the mound of cocoa beans in their sacks. Just for good measure, they were cutting the burlap with big hunting knives so the gasoline would have direct contact with the beans. Junior turned and went to the phone on his desk. He dialed 911.

"Yes, that's a good idea," Oliver Bodden said calmly. "We wouldn't want the fire to get out of hand, now would we."

A loud whoosh from outside brought Junior back over to the window, cordless phone in hand. The 911 operator answered as he and Oliver and Claude stared silently down at the mountain of burning cocoa beans. "Yes, operator. I want to report a fire at the Foster's Chocolate Factory. Yes, that's the correct address. No, it isn't life threatening, just . . . just some supplies, but hurry."

Claude grabbed Oliver Bodden by the tie and tried to shake him, a futile gesture as the older man was at least thirty pounds thinner than Oliver. "Who says it's not life threatening, you punk? How dare you destroy our property? You won't get away with this! You won't get away with any of this. This isn't some primitive country with a bunch of warlords killing each other . . ."

Junior Foster grabbed his brother's hands and Claude reacted by swinging his fist at his brother. He connected with Junior's chin solidly. Junior's head snapped and he let go of his brother's arms and touched his face gingerly. "You son of a bitch," Claude raged. "You got us into this. Now you better get us out of it."

Oliver Bodden was ambling away from them, like he didn't have a care in the world. "Learn from this little demonstration, gentlemen. And please don't involve me in your family fisticuffs. I'm sorry I can't stay for the fire department. I'm sure they'll find that it was a nasty case of arson. Some neighborhood kids, no doubt. You have no idea how it started, now do you?" He didn't even pause for a response. "I'm late for a dinner engagement. See you in the morning. My compatriots will see themselves out as well." He left the office.

The cocoa beans had become a raging inferno. But the bags had been placed on the concrete pad far from any other equipment and from the two wings of the factory. Nothing would be destroyed but the bags of beans. While two men watched the fire, the other four men had been busy parking all the forklifts in a neat line far to the side of the main building so they weren't involved in the conflagration. Now the men all disappeared around the new addition the way they had come in, silent and focused on getting out of there, but not running. They seemed to be used to this kind of work.

The sound of the fire truck sirens started in the distance.

Claude was staring, transfixed, at the flames. He came back with a little jump and turned from the window. "I'll call the insurance company," he said coldly, not apologizing to his brother for the punch, and walked out.

Junior went downstairs to meet the fire captain. It was going to be a long night.

Heaven moved along with the group as if she were on a conveyor belt. There was a bottleneck up ahead where Foster's Chocolate representatives were passing out press kits and trying to figure out if each guest was someone important or just a writer for the free apartment guide that folks read at the coffee shop. They'd invited anyone you could call "press" by any stretch of the imagination.

The crowd of about fifty people had been directed to the back of the plant, where a brand-new building stood. A side sliding door on this new building was partially open and Heaven could see rows of chairs set up. As they shuffled along, Heaven noticed the black stains on the concrete pad they were walking on. It looked like the site of a big bonfire. Heaven wondered if Foster's had come up with a new Kansas City wood-roasted flavor of chocolate just for all the barbecue lovers.

"Are you Heaven Lee?"

Heaven turned around to see who had asked. It was a pretty young woman with an official-looking Foster's Hostess badge. "How could you tell?" Heaven said with a smile and a glance at her kitchen clothes. "The person from your office asked me to wear my whites," she said by way of apology for her attire. Heaven did have on her chef's coat, a hot pink ski vest over it, some black-and-white striped baggy chef's pants and high heeled ankle boots in hot pink suede. The accessories helped.

"We have a special place for you all to sit, right next to the stage. Rick Bayless is here from Chicago and Dean Fearing from Dallas, I think. And the pastry chef from the American Restaurant," the hostess cooed as she slid Heaven out of the line and toward the open door of the plant.

"We chefs don't have to say anything, do we?" Heaven said in alarm. She was embarrassed enough wearing her professional clothes out in public.

"Oh, no," the young woman reassured her. "Mr. Foster will just talk about the event and the cookbook and have you stand up a minute. Are you shy in crowds?"

Heaven almost laughed. This woman obviously knew nothing about her. "No, I just like to know what's happening ahead of time." The woman deposited her in a chair next to the stage and glided away.

Heaven surveyed the room. Several big pieces of machinery were covered with white tarps. There must be more to this gig than the announcement of a charity event; either that or the artist Christo had been working here. She saw three reporters from the *Kansas City Star*, two people from the business desk as well as the food editor. The area set up for the press conference filled up fast. There were assorted print writers from local lifestyle magazines that Heaven recognized, plus three television camera operators and their talking head reporters, and of course, various city officials.

As people settled, more pretty women passed cups of coffee and chocolate chip cookies. Heaven snagged one as they went by, wondering why they were having baked goods instead of their own candy.

Then she leaned up to the next row of chairs to say hi to the pastry chef from the American. Soon, the two out-of-town chefs were seated next to Heaven by Miss Hostess and the four cooks got into a deep discussion about Oaxaca and the seven different mole sauces, most of which contained some chocolate.

The sound of microphone feedback from the small platform next to the chefs brought them back to the here and now.

"Hello, everyone," Junior Foster said to the crowd as he tapped the microphone nervously. It gave out another yelp of feedback. Someone jumped up on the stage and adjusted a knob under the tabletop podium, probably the guy who owned the PA system and rented it out for affairs like this.

"I'm Harold Foster, Jr., and this is my brother Claude." He indicated a gaunt man sitting next to him on the little stage. Brother Claude didn't look so good. "We sure have enjoyed celebrating the fiftieth year of Foster's Chocolates, the company our father started right here in Kansas City. Since our stock went public twenty-five years ago, the value of our company has increased tenfold and we're proud of that fact too. To top off the year, we're sponsoring a gala New Year's Eve Party at the Fairmont Hotel to benefit the food bank of Kansas City, Harvester's. There will be lots of food and two bands and for dessert, we'll be featuring the chocolate desserts of some of America's most renowned chefs." He looked over at the four people in chef's outfits. Heaven was embarrassed about the "renowned" part. She certainly didn't think she was in the same category with Rick Bayless. "These generous artists are each creating a new chocolate recipe for the evening and all the recipes will be printed in a cookbook. All the sales from the book will also benefit Harvester's. Representing the hundred chefs around the country who are participating are these four to my left. I'm sure you all recognize Kansas City celebrity Heaven Lee," Junior said, and Heaven got up and gave a big wave. Next the other three chefs were introduced and the crowd clapped. The camera operators shot a few feet of film, in case this turned out to be the big moment of the whole morning.

Junior motioned to some workers hovering at the back of the chairs. They started rolling two dollies forward, one on each side of the room. There were stacks of what Heaven recognized as ten-pound blocks of chocolate on them, but they were wrapped in a hot pink foil that Heaven didn't recognize. Miss Hostess and her crew, with big smiles, were passing these out to the assembled group.

Now the mayor had the microphone. "Until a year ago, I knew very little about the chocolate business. I still don't know much, but I do know that Foster's is the biggest boxed candy maker in America. Those guys back there in Hershey, Pennsylvania, beat Foster's out for sheer volume with their bar candy. But from now on, watch out, Hershey's." The mayor, a great speaker, was priming the pump. "Foster's is joining Hershey's in not only making great candy, but now Foster's will process their own cocoa beans, what is called second-tier chocolate production. This will provide two hundred new jobs for the Kansas City area." A nice round of applause greeted this news.

That means the city gave Foster's a big tax break on this new build-out, Heaven thought. She felt superior in her knowledge of the chocolate terms the mayor had bantered about since she'd already had a chocolate production lesson from Stephanie. She could actually follow along. From the looks on the faces of the rest of the crowd, most of them just understood the general drift that would lead their stories or be something they could brag about to their constituents: new jobs. "Now," the mayor said, wrapping up, "Harold Foster is going to give us a tour of the new operation so we'll know what the heck second-tier chocolate production means. Harold, thank you for placing this facility here in Kansas City." The mayor led the group in another round of clapping.

Junior Foster took the cordless mic back from the mayor. "Please take this commemorative block of Foster's semisweet chocolate home with you. Attached to it is the recipe for the wonderful chocolate chunk cookies you've been enjoying this morning, a recipe that will be in the Harvester's cookbook. Why don't you just leave your chocolate on your chairs for a few minutes while I show you how we made those ten-pound blocks." He stepped off the little platform. His brother and the mayor followed. Miss Hostess gestured to the chefs to fall in behind and they did, with everyone else straggling along. Two workers, big black men speaking to each other in a language Heaven didn't even recognize, removed the first tarp.

"The first step in turning cacao into chocolate is to roast the beans. This state-of-the-art oven roasts the beans at a low temperature, 100 to 150 degrees Celsius, or 212 to 302 degrees Fahrenheit. This brings out the chocolate flavor in the beans, much as roasting brings out the flavor in coffee beans," Junior explained as they hovered around the big ovens, the smell of chocolate strong in the air.

All of a sudden, someone goosed Heaven and she whirled around to find Sergeant Bonnie Weber standing behind her with an impish grin on her face. "Shhh," Bonnie said with a finger to her lips. She could just imagine Heaven using a loud and colorful phrase after that pinch. Heaven gave her an "I'll get even with you later" look and they walked on to the next station, where another tarp was being removed.

"This is the winnowing machine," Claude Foster reported. Heaven guessed the two brothers would be taking turns with the description duties. "It cracks open the seeds." Claude waited for a moment while the winnower did just that, then he showed the little morsels revealed inside. "The outer husks are sold for gardening and other purposes. These nibs, from West Africa, are then blended with nibs from other countries." Claude's head seemed to swivel around the room nervously as he described this process. When his eyes hit the big black men who were assisting, he visibly blanched, then he jutted his almost nonexistent chin out and continued. Was it a mild form of defiance? "The combination of different

nibs is what gives a chocolate house a distinctive taste."
Claude started moving toward another big machine that
was being unwrapped. He stole another glance around
the room. "Then we go to the grinder, or as it's called,
the melangeur, where the nibs are ground into a paste
called chocolate liquor." Huge granite rollers went into
action.

Before Claude could get it out of his mouth, some
reporter asked if there was alcohol in chocolate liquor.
While Claude was explaining there wasn't, Heaven
pulled on her friend's arm. "I guess I should have ex-
pected you to show up. Is this kinda like going to a
victim's funeral and slinking around to see who shows
up?" Heaven asked Bonnie.

Bonnie laughed. "A more tasteful version of that, yes.
If the shooter wasn't after the pilot, then he may be
planning some more nasty surprises for the company.
Or not. Maybe it was someone who hates shopping on
the Plaza. Anyway, I thought I'd show up, just for fun.
I'd hate it if our mayor got put in a hostage situation
and I wasn't around to save him."

Heaven stopped walking. "Did you get a threat?" she
asked.

"No way. If we'd gotten a real threat, this wouldn't be
such a casual appearance on my part and the mayor
wouldn't be here at all. Now stop asking me dumb questions and listen." Bonnie gave Heaven a little shove toward Junior, who had taken the mic back from his sickly
looking brother. Heaven noticed Claude heading away
from the crowd in a hurry.

Junior was explaining how Europeans only drank
chocolate mixed with sugar and spices for many years.
They couldn't understand the allure of eating grainy,

bitter, greasy chocolate until one of those clever Dutch men figured out this next step, the giant screw press to separate the cocoa butter from the solids. Everyone was suitably impressed as the hydraulic press smooched the chocolate liquor and substances came out two different troughs. Heaven guessed one was the heavier cocoa butter and the other was the cocoa. This machine reminded her of the cream separator that they used to have on the farm. She could see her father pouring the fresh, raw milk in the top of the machine, the cream oozing out of one spout, the milk rushing out of another spout into pails. The crowd shifted and Heaven came back to Earth.

"Now, we'll just step in the next area where the conching takes place. This process takes up to seventy-two hours and keeps smoothing the chocolate under heat in giant troughs." Of course someone asked why it was called conching and while Junior was explaining the term, another pair of foreign workers were opening a huge sliding metal door so the large group could move to the next room.

As the doors slowly opened, a ripple of sound started through the crowd. Sounds of concern and alarm. Before Heaven could see what had caused the oohing and ahhhing, Harold Foster cried out into the microphone, "Oh, no. How did *he* get there?"

The "he" was Oliver Bodden, although not many of the guests knew him from Adam. He was nattily attired in suit and tie, although not up to his usual impeccable standards. Oliver was in the conching machine, stuck like a rubber bath toy caught in the bathtub drain when the plug had been pulled on the bathwater. He bobbed silently as he was rolled over by giant metal tubes covered with melted chocolate. His eyes were closed. Right next to the giant machine stood Stephanie Simpson, holding a long piece of wire that was dripping not with blood but with the first batch of Foster's new chocolate.

Chocolate Truffles

½ cup heavy cream
8 oz. good quality semisweet chocolate, chopped fairly fine
2 T. flavored liqueur such as Grand Marnier, Irish Cream,
   cognac (optional)
½ cup cocoa, sifted

Bring cream to a boil in a heavy saucepan. In a mixing bowl, pour hot cream over chocolate and let stand for 5 minutes. Whisk until smooth. Add any flavored liqueur at this time. This is called ganache. Pour the ganache onto a nonstick baking sheet and put in the freezer for 15 minutes or in the refrigerator for 30–40 minutes. When the ganache is firm, form it into teaspoonsize balls. Drop truffles into the cocoa and roll around. Chill and store in an airtight container in the refrigerator for up to 2 weeks.

Six

I don't remember asking for you," Bonnie barked.

Heaven stood at the edge of the hallway outside Junior Foster's office door, now Bonnie Weber's temporary command post. "You didn't," Heaven snapped back, "but I'll be damned if I let you rip into Stephanie all by herself." Standing behind Heaven was Stephanie, tears in her eyes, her hands on Heaven's shoulders like a child hiding behind her mother. "And beside, I really need to get back to the restaurant. I told them I'd be gone for a couple of hours and it's been four. Can't we talk to you together?"

"Get in here. I'll start with both of you, but just know I might have to talk to ol' Stephanie, here, by herself."

Heaven and Stephanie hurried in and closed the door before Bonnie changed her mind. They both started talking at once, Heaven using her hands to gesture wildly and Stephanie shaking her head for emphasis.

"Stop!" Bonnie ordered, standing up and stretching her arms. Bonnie was tall, almost six feet, and she wore high heels to push her advantage further. Now she slipped off the dark red pumps. "Shit. My feet are killing me. If I'd known this would be a day-long ordeal, I woulda worn old shoes."

"Nice color," Heaven offered. "Are they Manolo Blahniks?"

Bonnie gave her a look and she shrank back and shut up.

"How are the tech guys doing?" Bonnie asked as she circled the desk and sat down on the edge of it close to where Stephanie perched on a straight-backed chair. Bonnie had moved Junior's comfortable visitor chairs back against the wall and found some uncomfortable straight-backed chairs in a storage room at the end of the hall and moved them into Junior's office.

"Still busy," Heaven piped up. "The chocolate is a problem for them in gathering evidence. And the poor uniforms who are taking statements. It was pretty funny watching all those reporters arguing who should be interviewed by your team first. They all wanted to get out of here and file a story in the worst way. Your guys had to threaten them all with detention time if they didn't form an orderly line and behave."

Bonnie chuckled. "They want to go write a big story, 'I saw a dead body at the chocolate factory.' Now, Stephanie, 'ol' buddy, do you want to tell me what made you decide to break the family feud and visit your uncles on this particular morning?"

Stephanie nodded her head, took a big gulp of air and started in. "Well, the other day when Heaven was at the store, she told me that Foster's was doing this big thing with all these famous chefs and that they'd asked her to be at this super important press conference and I just couldn't get it out of my mind."

"And so you decided to crash the party," Bonnie said, her arms crossed across her chest. "I've got that part. Now, how did you end up holding what I'd bet is the murder weapon over the body of poor old what's-his-name?"

"Oliver Bodden," Heaven said softly.

Bonnie didn't take her eyes off Stephanie, staring at her like the cobra gazing at the mongoose. "Over the body of Oliver Bodden. According to your uncle, he's a consultant to Foster's. Poor Oliver, who was dead and stuck in the conching machine, or perhaps killed in the conching machine, although I doubt that. This might be the damnedest of all these ridiculous food-related murders I've had to deal with—most of them because of you," she said with a look over her shoulder at Heaven.

Heaven wasn't going to bite this time. The more she talked back, the longer this would take. And she was just as curious as Bonnie to hear what explanation Stephanie would have. What was she doing there and why would she pick up something that obviously was a prime piece of evidence? Hadn't she learned anything about dead bodies and not touching weapons and stuff from hanging out with Heaven?

Stephanie, her usually perfect makeup job in complete disarray, dabbed at her mascara-mussed eyes with a tissue. "Well, I didn't know they'd built a new wing so I waited until everyone else had gone around to the back, then I went in the main part of the factory. I wandered around in there until someone assumed I was a member of the press who'd gotten lost, and they pointed the way to the new building. But I came in to the new building through the old building. The conching machine and the tempering station and the machine that forms the ten-pound chocolate blocks were all in that first section of the new wing. And you were all in the second section, the farthest part from the old factory. I heard my uncle talking and I started to go toward his voice. I could hear something thumping, the engine of the conching machine was obviously straining. So I went over there and . . ." Stephanie sniffled. "I looked down and saw the man and I bent closer to see who it was. I didn't recognize him, of course, but I spotted something else in the chocolate. The metal caught my eye and I just grabbed it, the wire I mean, and"—Stephanie gulped for air—"I didn't realize that it was still attached to the, uh, person's neck until just before the doors opened and I was face-to-face with the entire press establishment of Kansas City, plus the mayor and half the city council."

"If you're going to get caught, get caught big, I always say," Bonnie said.

Stephanie sniffed. "I swear, Bonnie—"

"Bonnie," Heaven cut in, "why in the world would Stephanie garrote some African chocolate expert she'd never laid eyes on before?"

"Why did someone kill the airship pilot? I bet the shooter had never laid eyes on him before either," Bonnie said with a shrug. "By the way, that's the official name for them: 'airship.' "

Heaven hadn't even thought about the fact that this was the second Foster's-related death in a week. "Oh, dear," she said. "I was so worried about Stephanie, I forgot about Sunday and the blimp."

"I bet the reporters didn't forget," Stephanie said peevishly.

"I bet you're right," Heaven said. "The reporters that got stuck with the boring press conference at some candy factory now get another murder with operatic overtones."

Bonnie shook her head. "Operatic overtones? Oh, brother. That's it for you. You're history. Get back to 39th Street right now."

"Don't you want to question me about what I saw?" Heaven asked defensively.

"I know what you saw because I was right beside you and saw the same thing. And I know there is no way to stop you from calling me several times this weekend with various wild theories about what all this means. Now go."

"Yeah, you were right next to me but did you see the puny Foster brother rush off in the middle of the tour?" Heaven asked, hoping to cast more doubt on Stephanie's potential guilt, not that she thought for a minute that Bonnie would try to pin this on Stephanie.

"The Foster brothers are next. They have lots to explain. Now go away," Bonnie commanded.

"Stephanie, did you call the people who work at your store? Are they okay? Do you want me to go down there and help them?" Heaven asked, doubtful that she would really be much help.

Bonnie shook her head. "That won't be necessary because Stephanie gets to leave too, in just a minute. Now, H, will you get?"

Heaven bent over and gave Stephanie a kiss on the cheek. "I wish I had a picture of you standing over the body with that wire in your hand, chocolate everywhere, your eyes bulging out."

Stephanie sniffed tragically. "I'm sure you'll see it on every station on the news tonight. The still photographers might not have been fast enough but the TV guys were already shooting film. I saw them aiming those awful cameras at me. No one will ever come to my store again."

"Nonsense," Heaven said. "Murder has always been good for my business. People are ghouls. You'll see." With that she left the office before Bonnie lost her temper.

What a morning. As she walked down the hall, trying to remember in which direction the stairs were, she heard agitated voices coming out of the office next to the one Bonnie was encamped in. She slowed down just to check it out. A few more seconds weren't going to make any difference at this point. When she'd called the café to report the latest dead body, the day crew sounded like they had it under control. Of course, that could change in a minute at a restaurant, when the chicken order doesn't show up or the dishwashing machine breaks again.

"Of course, I'm happy," admitted a voice that Heaven thought belonged to Claude Foster. "The man was an animal. He loaned us money to expand so he could ruin our company and take it over. But I guess what you're inferring is that because of all that, I killed him."

"Look, Claude, I'm just asking you straight out." Heaven took that voice to be Harold Foster's. "Do we have anything to worry about? You were pretty upset last night."

"Just because I punched my brother in the jaw for the first time in sixty some years, you think I went right on and took one of those wires we put around mailing crates—"

"Claude, calm down," Harold interrupted. "This will all be over soon. I think I've found someone to loan us the money to buy out West African Cacao."

"Who is it, someone from Columbus Park? Some mob guy?"

Heaven shifted uncomfortably outside the door. That was her neighborhood he was talking about. The remaining Italians were mostly sweet little old ladies.

"Claude, you're just going to have to get over this and trust me. Yesterday, I went downtown to the two locally owned banks that are left here. They understand the importance of keeping Foster's control in Kansas City. They said they would have financed the addition in the first place if I'd just . . . Well enough of that. Don't act dumb, Claude. You were there right beside me when we went to the Ivory Coast and you knew what we were doing."

"What makes you think they'll let go?"

"The so-called advisors told me they were flying home tonight, to get new instructions and take home the body of their boss. They said they wouldn't return until after the holidays. That gives us some time. I think they'll go for it because I'm going to offer them a premium to get out, that's why." Heaven could hear the resignation in Harold Foster's voice.

"Great, just great," his brother said bitterly, and before Heaven could get out of the way the door opened and the pale ghost, Claude Foster, stormed out, right into Heaven's rather curvaceous chest. "What in the world?" he thundered.

"What indeed!" Heaven said with disapproval, as if Claude had been trying to cop a feel. "I was just leaving the interrogation room. Has Sergeant Weber talked to you yet?"

Claude stopped his lion act and became the invisible man again. The reminder that there was still a police investigation to cope with made him shrink even further.

He continued down the hall without another word.

Heaven turned around to follow him and jumped. A stern-looking woman had appeared out of nowhere and looked like she was ready to take Heaven apart for eavesdropping.

"May I help you?" Marie Whitmer said frostily.

"No, no, just leaving," Heaven murmered.

Heaven made a beeline for the parking lot. She knew she should tell Bonnie what she'd just heard but it was Friday and her business needed her. She'd call her from the kitchen.

"Has Bonnie called me back yet?" Heaven yelled out to no one in particular.

The face of Murray Steinblatz popped up in the passthrough window from the kitchen to the dining room. "No is the answer, just like it was the answer ten minutes ago. Calm down, Heaven."

"I should have gone back in there and told her what I heard before I left the factory. She's going to yell at me."

"Heaven," Murray said, "from what little you've told me about what happened today, and what I heard on the radio in the car, Bonnie's got her hands full. She'll get back to you when she gets a minute. You don't honestly think Stephanie had anything to do with this guy ending up in the, what'd you call it?"

"Conching machine, and no, of course not. I think curiosity killed the cat, or in Stephanie's case curiosity made her a murder suspect. I don't know what killed Mr. Bodden. Since Stephanie herself has opened a chocolate business, I'm sure she's more interested in her mother's family business than she was when she was a lawyer's wife. So when I told her about this press conference, she just couldn't resist."

"Oh, so it's your fault?" Murray teased.

"As usual," Heaven said with a smile. The aroma of lemon oil perfumed the kitchen. She was intently poking a lemon with a fork, rolling it to get punctures all over it. Then she put it in the cavity of one of twenty chickens she was prepping for roasted lemon chicken.

Heaven asked the farmer she bought her poultry from to bring her pullets, hens just six weeks old, so she could serve them whole. She varied the preparation, sometimes roasting them with a sesame/soy/chili sauce glaze, sometimes with garlic and basil stuck under the skin, sometimes this way, with the flavor of lemon permeating the flesh. It was hard to find a good roast chicken in a restaurant in Kansas City so however they were presented, they sold out most nights. Heaven knew that lots of restaurants had chickens that had been precooked and then finished in the oven when they were ordered. This method usually meant that you didn't run out, but it also wasn't a truly fresh-roasted chicken. She took the chance on making it to the end of the evening with her fresh birds and tried to study the buying patterns of her customers to make sure she prepared enough. They usually sold thirty to forty chickens on Friday and Saturday nights. Jack was prepping the other twenty birds and they would go in the oven after Heaven's batch was finished and moved to the warming oven.

Heaven thought about Bonnie again. She really should know that the Foster brothers had a motive for getting rid of Oliver Bodden. It wasn't the kind of thing that the men were likely to have brought up to the detective on their own. She walked over to the phone and dialed. "Bonnie, by the time you get this I'll be unavailable, but we need to talk. Meet me at Sal's in the morning at nine. Okay, bye." She wished the detective had picked up but at least she'd made an attempt. She dialed again. "I know Stephanie can't talk but tell her to meet me at nine at Sal's. Oh, it's Heaven Lee," she said and hung up. Now she'd better get ready for the early guests who wanted to eat and get to a movie or the theater. She started setting up the saute station for the Friday night crowd.

Chocolate Espresso Pot de Crème

4 egg yolks, beaten and strained
1 cup half-and-half
½ cup whipping cream
3 oz. unsweetened baking chocolate
¾ cup espresso or very strong coffee
1 tsp. vanilla
pinch cinnamon

To strain the beaten egg yolks, use a wire mesh strainer, pushing the yolks through with your whisk or a spoon.

In a heavy saucepan, simmer half-and-half, cream, and chocolate until chocolate is melted and the mixture is smooth. Whisk in coffee. The mixture may separate but it will become smooth again. Simmer for 5 minutes, stirring occasionally.

Remove pan from heat, and add vanilla and cinnamon. Temper by pouring a quarter of the chocolate mixture into the eggs, whisking constantly until smooth. Return the egg mixture to the chocolate and whisk for about 3 minutes, until the pudding is no longer expelling steam.

Pour the custard in pot de crème containers, custard cups or chocolate cups, available at gourmet shops. Chill. Makes 4–6 servings.

Seven

Stephanie was finishing her news. "So, Janie, who never calls me, called to tell me that when she came in to work yesterday there were burned cocoa beans being thrown away. Janie says thousands of dollars worth."

Heaven nodded. "I saw a burned place on the brand new concrete palette. What's that about?"

"It was as if she was trying to tell me something that pointed to the brothers having a motive. But of course she did it in the most excruciating, roundabout way. I was so busy and she was totally unaware, as usual," Stephanie said.

"What's the deal on this cousin?" Bonnie asked as she carefully spread cream cheese on a bagel. Heaven had stopped for food supplies before she got to Sal's.

Stephanie finished a bite, then shrugged. "Janie's my aunt's only daughter. She went to the Kansas City Art Institute in graphic design, went to live in San Francisco for a while, then came back here when our uncle asked her to head up the graphics department for Foster's. My aunt had a fit, her being on the poor side of the family as I explained to you last week, but Janie said it was the best job she would ever be offered. Janie has a little self-image problem."

"How much do those sacks of beans cost?" Bonnie asked, knowing none of them would know the answer. "Why would anyone burn up their own inventory?"

"Did you ask the fire department if they had a call?" Heaven said, mouth full.

"Now what a good idea," Bonnie answered with plenty of sarcasm. "Since I just heard about this fire five minutes ago, I haven't had a chance to do that but now that you suggested it—" She pulled her cell phone out of the big purse she always carried and walked over to the door to talk privately.

Through all of this bagel eating and reporting, Sal had been busy with a ten-year-old's haircut, the first cut of the day. Sal had kept an eye on the proceedings through the mirrors on the walls of the barber shop. Now he paused and turned to the three women, his un-lit cigar wobbling in the corner of his mouth as he spoke. "So Heaven here hears the brothers talk about how the African guy is ripping them off but we don't know how. Then Stephanie's cousin, who works for this outfit, drops the news that some cacao beans was burned for no good reason. How do these two things get us any closer to the killer, that's what I want to know."

For a moment, the three women were quiet. Bonnie, who'd been following the conversation as she talked to the fire department, finished her call and put her phone back in her purse. Then they all started talking at once.

"Hush," Bonnie yelled quickly, and the other two reluctantly stopped talking. "Good question, Sal. That's why we like to have these think tanks over here at your joint, you ask good questions." The boy in the barber chair had brought his Walkman and was bouncing along to the Backstreet Boys, oblivious to the adult conversation. Bonnie looked at him to make sure he wasn't paying attention, then continued talking. "If Oliver was blackmailing or somehow conning the Fosters, that certainly goes on the motive page. Maybe the Fosters burned the cocoa beans themselves to prove a point to him."

"Or Oliver burned them to prove a point to the Fosters," Heaven said, excitement in her voice. "Then they were so mad, they strangled him and stuck him in . . ."

"Their brand new conching machine?" Stephanie said incredulously. "I don't think so. My uncles may be capable of taking financial advantage of their siblings, maybe—what am I saying, they *are* capable of that. But they wouldn't physically do harm, especially with a piece of wire. Ugh. Even if they hit him over the head first so he couldn't fight, it's hard for me to see them having the strength to strangle someone."

"Well, there was a knot on his head so you may have something there. Whoever did it might have knocked him unconscious first. But it also could have been caused by that big thingamajig, the conch gadget, banging into him," Bonnie said. "I do agree with Steph that the Foster boys seem more like the kind that let their lawyers do the dirty work." She stood up and checked her phone. "I wonder why the fire captain hasn't called me back. I am curious about that part of the story."

"Oh, Janie told me something else I didn't know about my family. My uncle David is already in town for the holidays. He arrived Thursday," Stephanie said.

"Just in time to kill Oliver but not in time to be the

airship sniper," Heaven observed, then realized how nonchalant she sounded about Stephanie's relative.

Bonnie got up. "He could always hire it out. I'll have to meet your other uncle. But not now. I'm going to be late for my daughter's soccer game if I don't get out of here. Sal, lovely of you to have us. Ladies, thanks for the info."

Heaven stood up too, brushing crumbs from her chef's jacket. "I have to get to work. They ate us out of house and home last night. Bonnie, I don't remember you sharing much information with us. Don't think I didn't notice that."

"I'm supposed to be the information gatherer, remember?" Bonnie said as she went out the door.

Stephanie went over to the newspaper on one of the chairs and picked up the front page, the one featuring her photo holding the wire. The angle of the shot hid the actual contents of the machine beside her. "I was wrong about the still photographers being slow."

Heaven took the paper out of her hand and waved at Sal as she pushed Stephanie out the door. They stood on the sidewalk for a minute. Heaven patted her friend's arm. "Are you okay?"

Stephanie nodded. "This working for a living is a bitch. We are so busy and I know I have to make money now so I can pay my rent in January and February, but I'm whipped and the busiest day of the week is on top of me and I'm a murder suspect of someone I never saw alive."

"Stop whining and have a profitable day," Heaven ordered.

Stephanie nodded. "When I found out Uncle David was in town, at my grandmother's, I called him and begged him to help. He's going to work the cash register."

Heaven was already exiting the bonbon shop. She gave Stephanie a thumbs-up and headed across 39th Street to the café as Stephanie gave her a pitiful wave and then got in her car. Heaven went right in the front door and out the back, stopping just long enough to check the prep list and make sure everyone had come to work that morning. The café wasn't open for lunch on Saturdays so the kitchen crew was working at a slightly easier pace than on the weekdays. "I have an errand to run," she said to no one in particular. Everyone looked up and nodded, busy at their stations. She went out the back to her van, jumped in and headed for the Plaza.

While Bonnie, Stephanie and Heaven had been talking over the latest Foster's Chocolate murder, Heaven had had a brilliant idea about the first one. All of a sudden she remembered an old friend of hers from Kansas had recently moved to one of the big apartment buildings just north of the Plaza's main drag. He'd moved to the penthouse. Heaven pulled in the circle drive and left the keys in the car.

The doorman, a rare bird in Kansas City, came to the door. "I'd love to see Dale Traver, if he's home," Heaven said before he could ask her business.

He opened the foyer up and went to a house phone and dialed. "Who shall I say is calling?"

"Heaven, ah, Katy O'Malley," Heaven said, using her maiden name for a change. Dale was an antique dealer whom she had met years ago with her parents. He still thought of her as Katy.

The doorman got an answer and in a minute put the phone down. "You can go right up. Top floor," he said as he opened the inner door and gestured toward the elevators. There was an arrangement of silk flowers in the lobby on a credenza.

"I bet Dale hates these," Heaven muttered as she touched them lightly as she passed.

When she got to the penthouse level, Dale was standing at the elevator door, waiting to greet her. "What in the world brings you here on a Saturday morning?" he said as he held out his arms and gave her a big hug.

"I guess I can't just say I was in the neighborhood, can I?"

"Not with any success." Dale took Heaven's arm and they went in to the apartment.

"Wow," Heaven said, truly impressed for a change. The place was gorgeous, full of lovely French nineteenth century furniture mixed with art deco pieces, oriental rugs, and a great collection of old portraits from the eighteenth and nineteenth centuries. The rooms reflected the kind of eclectic taste that Heaven also had, only Dale's was worked out on a more expensive scale. Dale himself was an elegant silver-haired man, dressed in a Harris tweed sports jacket and dark green corduroy pants.

"Would you like some coffee?" Dale asked, a mischievous grin on his face.

"Yes, but what are you looking at me like that for? You look like the cat that swallowed the canary," Heaven said as she went toward a beautiful silver service that just happened to be on the sideboard of the dining room with coffee and a plate of scones sitting nearby.

If he didn't know I was coming, maybe he was expecting someone else, Heaven thought. Maybe someone else was here. Maybe that's why he's smiling so funny. "Dale, were you expecting someone else? Have I interrupted something?"

Dale poured her a cup. "You take cream, no sugar, right?" He handed her the cup and slipped a tiny scone and a chocolate truffle on the saucer. "You're sure full of questions. Let's take them in order. I was smiling at you because I have a feeling you're investigating one of your famous cases. I can just feel it. I look like the cat that swallowed the canary because I have a feeling you're going to ask for my help. No, I wasn't expecting anyone and you didn't interrupt a thing except me reading the *Star*, which didn't take long. I use my silver and my good china all the time. I'm not getting any younger and I'm not saving them for a special occasion. I enjoy using my beautiful things." He sat down on a big, down-filled couch and patted a place next to him. "Now, what is it? An antiques scam of some kind?"

Heaven sat down and hoped she wouldn't disappoint Dale, since she had no antique scam to consult about. "Do you remember last Sunday, when the blimp crashed and the pilot was shot?"

Dale shook his head sadly. "Kids with guns. I tell you, how that Charlton Heston can hold up his head when these kids go around shooting off these high-powered rifles in the heart of town, killing their classmates and now, some poor airship pilot."

Heaven perked up. "What makes you think it was a kid? Did you see anyone?"

"No, that's just a grumpy old man talking, Katy. I was going to an afternoon performance of the Nutcracker Ballet last Sunday with some friends and I got caught up in the traffic jam that happened after the shooting and was twenty minutes late."

"Oh," Heaven said with disappointment in her voice, "so you weren't here. I thought . . . Let me tell you what I thought. This is a pretty high building and I thought maybe you saw someone going up on the roof. They'd have to have come up this way, wouldn't they?"

"You think a sniper used this building to pick off the Foster's Blimp?" Dale said with barely concealed excitement.

"But I guess you didn't see anything, before you left for the ballet?" Heaven asked again.

"No, dear, no one came up here with a deer rifle and camo gear. The only person I remember was a Santa Claus photographer, waiting for the elevator when I came down."

Alarms went off in Heaven's head. "Wait a minute. Someone in a Santa suit was waiting for the elevator to go up? How do you know he was a photographer?"

"He had two cameras around his neck and one of those big silver Halliburton suitcases that photographers use," Dale said with a slight amount of pique in his tone. He knew a photographer when he saw one.

"You didn't happen to talk to him, did you?"

"I said something like, 'Oh, I suppose someone's having a child's Christmas party,' and he smiled and nodded and got on the elevator. Nice idea, having a Santa that also takes photos of the little ones," Dale said.

"So you never actually heard the Santa talk? And you don't have any idea what floor he was headed for, do you?"

"No, but I know almost everyone in the building. Do you want me to ask around?"

Heaven got up and popped the last bite of the truffle in her mouth. "Would you, please, Dale?"

He stood up and gave that cute smile again. "Are you working with the police on this, or is it your own investigation?"

"My friend Bonnie Weber in the police department is heading this case, and also the death that happened at the Foster's factory yesterday. I just happened to be around when both of the, uh, incidents occurred," Heaven said as she walked toward the door with her arm intertwined with Dale's. "I think she sent uniforms around to all these buildings after the blimp was shot down. But you weren't home to tell them about the mysterious camera-toting Santa."

"Well, I don't know how mysterious he was but I'm glad to be part of Heaven's G-men." Dale chuckled and gave Heaven a peck on both cheeks, European style.

"I'm sure this will be a waste of your time. I'd go with you up and down the halls but I've got to get back to work. We have lots of reservations tonight."

"Don't you worry about me. I have plenty of time to waste. But Katy, or Heaven as you call yourself now, from what I've read and what you've said, someone is either out to make trouble for Foster's, or it could be to make trouble for you."

"Don't be silly. It was just a coincidence that I was around both times." She hoped she sounded convincing. The thought that it was directed at her had crossed her mind. She'd dismissed it, of course, as paranoid thinking. Not everything bad that happened in Kansas City was about her.

"Wow," Joe Long said as he walked into Heaven's kitchen/living room. "Good tree."

"I know. Hank got it last Sunday, not at the last minute like I usually do because I'm feeling conflicted about using up our natural resources for my own pleasure. He told me that particular tree was grown to be consumed, just like a carrot. He was very persuasive." Heaven was looking around for her bag and coat.

95

"How Zen, I think," Joe said. "What are you looking for?"

"My coat and stuff. I was so tired last night when I got home I just threw them down." She was doubled over the back of a couch, butt up, pulling on the sleeve of a bright yellow down-filled long coat that had slid on the floor. "And after that I threw myself down on this couch and watched the Christmas tree until I fell asleep, which didn't take very long. My coat must have slipped over the edge." She pulled a faux python bag big enough to live out of for a weekend from the same spot as the coat, then stood up and got bundled up. "I was worn out. We were busy."

Joe nodded. "Thank God. I made two hundred dollars last night and not a moment too soon. I haven't bought one gift yet. After this contest, and of course, after we eat something, I think I'll go shop for an hour or so. I'm sure it won't take that long to spend two hundred bucks. Where's Hank and how come you slept on the couch?"

"Hank, being the mensch that he is, is working all weekend in the emergency room so some doctor friend of his can get married. I didn't sleep there all night, just until three or so when I woke up and went up to bed."

Joe smiled. "It's funny hearing you use that Jewish word for a Vietnamese American Catholic. But it's certainly appropriate. Hank is the nicest guy."

"I know. I don't deserve him," Heaven said as she locked the door and followed Joe to his rusted out pickup truck. "Are you sure you don't want me to drive?"

"No, it's my friend and her body building contest and it's already cost you one evening and a hefty bar tab on the house. At least let me drive and pay for breakfast, or brunch or whatever."

"What time is the contest?" Heaven asked.

"Noon in the first floor of the building with the movie theaters upstairs that used to be called Seville Square. A tacky mall atmosphere if you ask me, but I guess they were able to get the Plaza to pay for some advertising for the body builders. The Santa contest that was postponed from last week is going on in the same space after the body builders so it should be a real visual circus. I hope none of the Santa contestants are also in the body building contest."

"Well, that would be a stretch, since the body building is for women and the Santas are men."

Joe wagged his finger. "It's the twenty-first century and I'm sure there'll be some women in the Santa contest. And you saw those muscley women. Except for the Santa belly, some of them could pass."

"Yeah, what am I thinking? Your friend's gender was challenged. How did that turn out anyway? I felt sorry for her. It was kind of humiliating."

Joe pulled into an empty space in the parking garage near the building they were headed for. "I felt sorry for Kathy too," he said. "She took her lover's death real hard last year and she put her energy into this body building. It was something they did together so it means a lot to her. All I know about that gender test is she called and said she was cleared to be in the competition and would love it if you and I could be there to cheer her on. I think she might have a little crush on you. You were so nice to her the other night."

"Well, if she mentions a little crush to you, I'm depending on you to nip it in the bud. Just tell her what a die-hard hetero I am."

Joe laughed. "I'll just tell her about all of your husbands."

"By the way, how did you and Kathy meet?"

"At my gay and lesbian consciousness raising group," Joe said sheepishly. He knew Heaven thought too much introspection was dumb.

"Oh, brother. I'm sorry I asked," Heaven chuckled.

They hurried across the street to a three-story building. Housing a movie theater, the building also had a large enclosed space bordered with shops. This indoor plaza was the site for various concerts and personal appearances of soap stars and the like. Today it was crowded with the participants and fans of the body builders and Santas.

When they joined the crowd, the contest was already underway. A group of nine women, Kathy included, lined up on a temporary stage with a small catwalk. They were wearing bikinis and lots of oil and one by one, they stepped front and center and flexed their arms to the applause of the crowd.

Heaven was more interested in the Santas, who were slowly showing up around the stage to watch the first contest of the day. She studied each bewhiskered face, still working on the theory of a Santa being the shooter last Sunday.

She knew if a Santa had done in the airship, the chances of him coming back in costume this Sunday were slim. But she also knew lots of these nuts got off on flaunting themselves in the face of authority, putting themselves in dangerous situations, so maybe the shooter had come back dressed as Santa this Sunday, just to make it more fun.

Nothing set off her internal alarms, not that she'd laid eyes on the imagined Santa shooter to recognize him again. Heaven depended on her intuition to lead her but this group all looked so sweet in their red suits and white beards. Even the Rasta Santa had an innocent demeanor.

Joe punched Heaven's arm. "The woman that was giving Kathy a hard time last week, she seems like she's in trouble."

Heaven turned her attention to the body builders. They were showing off their backs now, stepping to the end of the catwalk, turning back out with their hands on their hips then popping every muscle from their shoulders to their waist. This was a showy pose and the crowd loved it. Heaven saw the woman Joe had been talking about, the one who had been giving Kathy trouble at the health club. She was pale and wobbling, sweat pouring down her neck as she waited her turn to pose. Heaven moved closer to the stage. She was up next and staggered as she came forward. The crowd started a murmur that turned into a steady hum of concerned voices. They were concerned but also titillated by the possibility of some kind of problem on stage. The contestant turned her back to the crowd, and then, instead of pulling herself taut she crumpled into a heap on the stage floor. Heaven turned to check out Kathy's reaction and wasn't surprised to see her smile. Tit for tat. This was a ruthless bunch.

Quickly, with the help of two other contestants and a nurse who must have been on call, the woman was helped off stage. She was sobbing and as she passed Kathy, she lunged at her. She had enough energy to get her hands around Kathy's neck but then she caved in again, clinging to Kathy and choking out, "You did this to me, you bitch, you—"

Kathy pushed her back in the arms of the two people assisting her with a savage grin. "Looks like I'm up here and you're not."

The nurse promptly sat the sick woman down in a straight-backed chair by the side of the stage and checked her pupils and blood pressure. Heaven heard the nurse ask her if she had hypoglycemia, and she muttered something that Heaven couldn't hear.

The contest went on through two more body parts and Heaven turned her attention back to the stage. The next time she glanced toward the sick bay, the chair was empty and the nurse was writing on a form stuck on a clipboard. Heaven strolled over to the nurse. "I hope that contestant is going to be all right. What was the matter?"

The nurse shrugged. "It happens quite a bit at these things. They don't eat before a competition. Then you add nervousness and the amount of vitamins these girls take. It's a wonder they don't all puke."

"Was she sick?" Heaven asked.

"Oh, yeah. I always have some barf bags ready."

"So you work these contests often?"

The nurse, herself with a soft, padded body, nodded. "I guess that tells you something, doesn't it. That you have to have a nurse on hand for a body building contest says a lot."

"It isn't something you'd figure on a nurse for, now that you mention it," Heaven said sweetly. "Not like a skateboarding contest. After all, they're just standing there." She glanced up to see some kind of a grand pose-off going on up on stage, each one of the women going through a variety of poses. The crowd was enthusiastic, clapping and whistling.

"Getting a body to that point of perfection, if that's what you want to call it, causes a lot of stress on the body and the body builder, if you know what I mean," the nurse said. Just then a contestant came rushing off stage, red in the face, gasping for water. The nurse quickly squirted water in her mouth from a plastic bottle and the body builder ran back up the stairs.

Heaven moved away, looking around for the sick girl. Kathy had mentioned last week she was a crowd favorite. Now the crowd had forgotten her for the moment and she was puking and shaking in the bathroom some-where. Was she right about the ruthlessness of compe-tition and had Kathy dosed her sports drink with something? Or was the nurse right and it was just part of the game?

The winners were being announced and Kathy was named reserve champion, which as far as Heaven could tell was first runner up. That seemed very good for a woman who was probably ten years older than anyone else on the stage. While the photos were being taken, Heaven slipped into a couple of shops. She emerged with two big sacks.

"Did you cross someone off your Christmas list, you dog?" Joe asked. He and Kathy were ready to depart, it seemed. Kathy had on some sweats, a coat, and was lug-ging her trophy proudly.

"No, I just got us three toys so we could vote at the Santa contest. Kathy, congratulations."

"Thanks, Heaven. I'm sure glad that's over. Joe asked me to join you for lunch, if that's okay. I'm starved."

Heaven guided the other two over to a large trash container that was filling up with toys. "I'm starved too, but this won't take long. I've just got to see the Santas strut their stuff. They're lining up now. I read the sign that says a donation for the Toys for Tots program gets you a vote, so I bought us a stuffed animal, a checker-board set and an infant toy of some kind that plays music."

"Thanks for getting these. I'll pay you back," Kathy said as they gave their toys to a volunteer who then handed them a ballot. "It'll be fun to watch someone else sweat through a contest for a change."

Heaven could hardly wait to grill Kathy about the incident on stage. But she kept her mouth shut for the time being while they got some laughs out of the Santas.

Every Santa had their own music and they walked the catwalk to everything from "Jingle Bells" to a Calypso version of "I Saw Mommy Kissing Santa Claus" played on steel drums. Then each Santa had to answer a question, something about if he could have one gift, what would he ask for. It was just like the Miss America contest. Heaven could see this was going to take another hour.

"What do you say we make a snap judgment on beauty alone and go eat?"

Joe and Kathy nodded and they marked their ballots and handed them to the volunteer.

"So, who did you two vote for?" Joe asked as they headed for the door.

"I went with the traditional, the guy with the real beard that was so perfect," Kathy said.

"And I had to go with the fashion victim, the one with the tie-dyed outfit with the rhinestones and the high tops instead of boots," Heaven confessed.

"I voted for the one with the Marie Antoinette wig, of course," Joe said as if it were a foregone conclusion.

They headed into the Classic Cup and Charlene Welling, the owner, took them to the front of the line, ignoring the dirty looks of the other patrons who were waiting. When they were seated by the window, just one table from where Heaven had dined last week with Stephanie, Heaven shivered involuntarily.

"What? Are you afraid one of those holiday shoppers will attack us for getting to a table before them?" Joe asked, glancing back at the line.

"No, I was sitting right there," Heaven pointed to the table to their right, "last week, when all of a sudden, people started running and we heard shots and then the blimp came down and right after that, the pilot bit the dust."

"Yeah, that was quite a deal," Kathy said. "What do you think, someone practicing with their new deer rifle?"

Joe shook his head. "Not in the middle of the Plaza. Then Heaven was at the press conference at the Foster's plant on Friday when some big shot from Africa was found murdered. Two bad things in the same week. It can't be an accident. I think someone wants the fiftieth year of Foster's Chocolate to be the last."

A basket of muffins had appeared. Heaven grabbed a lemon-poppyseed version and slathered it with whipped butter. "But enough of boring old snipers and stabbings, let's get to the good stuff. What happened with your gender test?"

Kathy looked away, her good humor gone.

For a moment, Heaven wanted to cut her own tongue out. But since she'd already opened her big mouth, she waited for an answer. She stuck a muffin in Kathy's hand and smiled expectantly.

"The exam was short and hurt my pride more than anything. The doc was cool. She asked me if I'd changed gender, if I'd been a man earlier in my life. I told her I'd been a mother earlier in my life and she got a kick out of that. She took some blood and then did a pelvic and surprise, surprise, I'm a female. They can create a vagina out of nothing but they can't create a cervix and stuff."

Joe paled visibly at such intimate girl talk. These were not parts he was familiar with.

Their food had arrived. Heaven had stuck with breakfast, eggs Benedict, Kathy had gone for lunch, grilled salmon, and Joe was having both, pancakes and a grilled chicken club sandwich.

"So," Joe asked casually, like he was asking about a recipe, "what did you do to that woman today to get even? She was a mess. Did you put a laxative in her sports drink?"

Kathy looked genuinely shocked. "I didn't do a thing to her. She may not take body building and the competitions seriously, but I do, and I wouldn't do to her what she did to me."

"So, if you weren't responsible," Heaven asked, "and I have to tell you I wouldn't blame you if you were, what was the matter?"

"It happens. I've never seen Jane fold like that, but she probably had low blood sugar. No food, the pressure, lots of B vitamins and some other supplements, and all of a sudden, you start to sweat and your stomach turns and you get dizzy. I've had the same experience."

"What do you do so you don't get sick?" Heaven asked as she stole a bite of pancake from Joe's side of the table.

"I get up early and eat something. It's ridiculous to take a lot of strong vitamins on an empty stomach. But some of these girls think the bacon and eggs will show up on the side of their bodies in a big lump."

Heaven pushed her plate away after that image. It was empty anyway. "I admire you for not wanting to get even. Why was—did you call her Jane?—why was she on your case?"

Kathy shrugged. "Jane Anderson is a nutcase. I think she's a former fat kid. Or a former anorexic. I can tell she has issues around food. And she works for a food company. Ironic, isn't it?"

"Oh, yeah? Which one?" Heaven said idly. She wanted a nap.

"Foster's."

Joe and Heaven both perked up. "Foster's Chocolate?" Joe asked. "What does she do?"

"I have no idea," Kathy replied.

"Isn't life funny," Heaven said. "I've never thought much about Foster's until about two weeks ago when they called me and asked me to create a dish for this New Year's Eve celebration. Now every day something happens that involves Foster's, even at a body building contest. I feel like I'm being stalked by Foster's."

"I wish we had some right now—chocolate, that is, not stalkers," Joe said as he got up and threw a wad of money down. "Anyone want to go Christmas shopping with me?"

Heaven got up and hugged both Kathy and Joe. "I'm going for a nap. Kathy, congratulations. Joe, thanks for brunch. Go around to Stephanie's if you're hungry for chocolate. She has these new treats, an espresso chocolate pot de crème in a chocolate cup. They rock."

"Good idea. How are you getting home, though? We came together."

"I know that but I'm calling a cab. You stay here and shop."

Joe gestured to Kathy. "Let's go have some chocolate, reserve champion."

Kathy held her trophy over her head, much to the amusement of the rest of the café crowd. "Okay, then I'm taking this baby home," she said with a big smile.

Rabbit in Sweet Sour Sauce

2 rabbits, each cut in six pieces
2 onions, sliced
2 cloves garlic, crushed
2 stalks celery, diced
1 bay leaf
3 sprigs rosemary, finely chopped
3 sprigs sage
2 sprigs parsley
1–2 bottles red wine
Salt and pepper to taste
½ cup olive oil
2 T. butter
Flour for dredging
2–3 T. sugar
½ cup red wine vinegar
2 oz. bitter chocolate, chopped
⅓ cup pine nuts
⅓ cup golden raisins

Marinate the rabbit overnight in the vegetables, herbs, 1 bottle wine, salt and pepper. Drain and reserve the marinade.

Heat the oil and butter in a heavy saute pan. Dredge the rabbit in flour and brown. Add the marinade and simmer gently for 1–2 hours, depending on the size of the rabbit pieces.

Dissolve the sugar in the vinegar over a low heat. Add the chocolate, pine nuts, and raisins. Then add this to the pan sauce and simmer together for 5 to 10 minutes. If you don't like a chunky sauce, you can drain all the sauce off the rabbit, blend it with an immersion mixer, and then add the sweet sour mixture. The vegetables will be pureed and the only chunky elements will be the nuts and raisins. I've done it both ways and it's very good in either style.

Eight

It was Wednesday, December 20th, the day Iris would arrive in Kansas City. Heaven was looking forward to it and dreading it all at the same time. She so wanted her daughter home but didn't want to share their time together with Stuart Watts. She was also nervous about her ability to refrain from smarting off at Stuart and thus making her daughter angry. Iris had grown to adulthood without them going through the period of alienation that some mothers and daughters experienced. Heaven didn't want to blow it now. So she filed the imminent arrival in the back of her mind and concentrated on Foster's instead.

She parked her van in the parking lot of the Foster's plant. For days she'd been thinking about what had happened on Friday. Who was the dead man really, besides someone the Foster brothers were glad to be rid of, and why had he ended up in the conching machine?

She'd attempted contact with Bonnie but every time she called, the sergeant was out of the office or in a meeting. Heaven thought things must be breaking fast for Bonnie not to call her back, either that or she was avoiding Heaven's theories. The only thing left to do was come to the scene of the crime herself on some flimsy excuse and hope to find some answers.

And as an extra added bonus she was going to look up Jane the body builder. She knew she was just being nosy, but at least it would keep her mind occupied so she didn't have time to fret about Stuart Watts.

Heaven made a beeline for the offices of Claude and Harold. She'd called ahead and found out they were at a meeting and wouldn't return to the plant until ten o'clock. It was now 9:30. That gave Heaven thirty minutes to talk to the help. She figured she'd get more information from them than from the big shots.

"Oh, hello," Heaven said to the secretary who seemed to work for both the Foster brothers. Her desk was positioned between their two offices. She was the bulldog that had caught Heaven listening to the brothers at their office door. As they had never been officially introduced, Heaven decided to ignore that encounter. "I'm Heaven Lee, one of the chefs participating in the New Year's Eve chocolate party. I called Claude, or was it Harold, and told him, whichever him it was, I'd pop down today. I have a few delicious ideas for the event."

The secretary, a matronly looking woman who actually had her hair back in a bun, looked at her blankly. "When did you call? I don't remember a call."

Heaven gave her a big smile, playing a happy airhead. "Monday, or was it Tuesday? I'm sure your phone has been ringing off the hook, what with the unfortunate accident on Friday. I was here for the press conference, you know."

The secretary bit. "I remember you," she said tersely.

"But accident? I don't know how you'd call it an accident when Mr. Bodden had a mile of wire wound around his neck, or at least before the brothers' niece showed up and pulled it off."

"Who was Mr. Bodden again?" Heaven asked in an unconcerned voice, like she really didn't care and was just being polite.

The secretary's face clouded up. Her look indicated there was something about the deceased she hadn't liked. "Well, when the brothers—we all call them 'the brothers'—decided they wanted to process the chocolate, not just make the candy, they went to several cacao growers, I think mainly in West Africa but they also went to Mexico, I recall. They were looking for someone who wanted to be able to take their product from the tree to the box to partner with them. Mr. Bodden was it."

"Oh, I get it, cut out all the middlemen, eh?"

The secretary looked proud, then the pride disappeared from her eyes. "That was the idea."

Heaven saw something to pick at. "But I'd guess by the fact that Mr. Bodden turned up dead that it didn't work out like that."

Alarm. The secretary took her defensive position, arms spread out from one side of the desk to the other, fingers locked on either corner as if Heaven was going to try to go through her drawers, looking for evidence. "The brothers, Harold and Claude Foster, have been my employers for twenty-two years and I have never seen them solve a problem with violence of any kind," she said with pursed lips.

"No, of course not," Heaven said reassuringly. "I saw some other Africans here on Friday. It could be some old feud from back home. Maybe someone saw this as a good time to settle a score. Or there's always random violence to blame nowadays. But I get the impression that you didn't think the partnership was going well, before the, eh, unfortunate event on Friday."

The secretary shook her head firmly. "No, I think Mr. Bodden wasn't the honest person that the brothers thought he was. I surely didn't like the way he started acting like he owned the place. And then there was the fire."

Heaven tried not to salivate. Stephanie's cousin had been right to think the fire had something to do with all the trouble. "Well, now that you mention it, on Friday I noticed a big, black, sooty place out on the slab between the buildings. Did that have anything to do with the fire?"

The secretary leaned forward conspiratorially. "Thousands and thousands of dollars of cocoa beans, up in flames. The brothers say it was just vandalism, that some kids climbed over the fence and set a fire, but those beans aren't stored out there in the middle of the yard where they'd be exposed to the weather. You can't tell me a bunch of kids took the time to move dozens of sacks of cocoa beans that weigh a ton just so they could play a destructive prank. I think that Oliver Bodden had something to do with it, although I can't for the life of me figure out why anyone in the business would do such a thing, destroying expensive product. I smell a rat."

Bingo. The theory that they'd started developing at Sal's was seeming more and more likely, but there still wasn't an apparent reason that Heaven could see for Bodden or the Fosters to burn the beans. Before she could ask the secretary for more of her theory, the brothers swept around the corner deep in conversation. When they saw Heaven, they froze and blinked, both looking like the proverbial deer in the headlights.

Heaven could almost see them trying to remember who in the heck she was.

"Hi, gentlemen. Heaven Lee, remember? I'm one of your chefs. And I called and talked to one of you the other day and said I had some wonderful ideas for the New Year's Eve gala."

The two men stared at each other, each trying to recollect a call that, of course, Heaven had never made. She smiled cheerfully but tried to indicate a firmness of will. She wanted them to know she wasn't going away until they listened to her scintillating ideas.

Harold broke first. "I'm sorry if you've been waiting long, Heaven. Our lives have been turned topsy-turvy by this situation . . . the murders. I'd love to think about something more cheerful for a while. Come into my office, won't you?"

Claude looked with relief at his brother for taking on this chore and nodded, turning to his office. The secretary gave him a stack of phone messages as he passed her desk.

Heaven's wheels were turning fast. How could she slide the conversation from New Year's Eve to cocoa beans and Oliver Bodden, especially when Harold had indicated he was sick to death of those topics? She thought of a novel approach: telling the truth, or at least a portion of it.

"I'm not trying to interfere, but I have to tell you something," Heaven said as she sat down across the desk from Harold.

That got Harold's attention. "Please don't tell me you can't participate after all on New Year's Eve."

"No, this is actually not about New Year's Eve. It's a confession. On Friday I accidentally heard you and your brother talking privately, when I was leaving this office after my turn with the detective. You know how a little knowledge can be a dangerous thing? Well I've been worried about what I heard and I decided I should just ask you about it."

The man rubbed his temples with one hand. "I have no idea what we were talking about a few minutes ago, let alone on Friday. My brain has turned to mush. Give me a clue."

"You asked your brother if he killed Oliver Bodden, not in exactly those words, but that's what you wanted to know. He said the, eh, victim was trying to take over your business, that he hated him and was glad he was dead but he didn't kill him. You mentioned getting someone to finance buying the African Cacao Company, or a name to that effect, out of your business. He mentioned punching you for the first time in your lives." She said it all in a rush, then sat quietly, eyebrows raised.

Harold drew himself up. "I don't want you to think that I doubted my brother's innocence. I feel responsible for the mess we're in right now. I am the one who sought a partnership with Oliver Bodden's company, West African Cacao Company is the correct name. I had no idea that Mr. Bodden would be less than forthcoming with us until a few days before his death. The circumstances do not look good, I grant you. But I can tell you without any doubt that Claude and I did not take things into our own hands."

"What about the fire?" Heaven said, knowing she was pushing it.

Heaven watched Harold Foster try to figure out where this was going. Some vague memory of seeing Heaven before, perhaps at the press conference or even in their offices that day in the chaos that followed, flashed across his face. Or maybe he even recognized her name from reading about her previous exploits in the newspapers. Then she saw suspicion and anxiety appear in his eyes. What, did he think she was some kind of nut, some kind of murder magnet? Or worse yet, did he think she could somehow be responsible for the problems besieging their company? But before he could decide how to answer her question about the fire, the secretary burst in the door. "You better come out here, Junior. The police are here."

Heaven and Harold Foster got to the door just in time to see Bonnie Weber and two uniformed policemen walk out of Claude's office. Claude was handcuffed and walking between the two officers. Bonnie looked surprised to see Heaven.

"Bonnie, what's going on?" she asked.

"Manslaughter, H. Mr. Foster, I'm sure you'll want to get a lawyer for your brother. We'll be downtown. I'm not sure when the arraignment will take place, but we won't start without you." Bonnie held out her hand as if to stop the onset of questions she could feel coming her way from Heaven. "Heaven, don't start. I'll talk to you later."

"Junior?" Claude said softly.

"Don't worry, brother," Harold said and turned back to his office to start making calls.

And then Bonnie and her prisoner were gone, leaving Heaven and the secretary staring after them.

Heaven was sitting in her car in the Foster's parking lot. She had made nice upstairs, saying she was sure Harold would be able to straighten the whole thing out for Claude, saying how sorry she was, saying a few other inept platitudes, then giving the secretary her card and telling her to call her if she could be of help, as if there was anything at all she could do.

The whole thing made her wish she was still able to practice law, not that she was ever the criminal defense attorney that Claude needed now.

As she sat there regretting the past for a minute, a car pulled up beside her, and what do you know, the body builder Jane got out, gathering a group of papers from her back seat.

Heaven jumped out of her van and the woman looked up. "I'm sorry to be so bold, but I think I saw you Sunday at the body building contest," Heaven said in her most nonthreatening voice. There was no good way to bring up a public event in which you make a fool of yourself. "I'm Heaven Lee, by the way. I'm one of the chefs for the New Year's Eve chocolate party." Boy, had she used that line to cover a multitude of sins today. "I'm glad to run into you. I was concerned about your health."

"Yes, it was a big disappointment. It must have been something I ate the night before," Jane said with a grim little smile. "I'm fine now."

She didn't mention another body builder sabotaging her. "What's your name?" Heaven asked bluntly. She'd told her name, now it was time for Jane Anderson to do the same. After all, she didn't know Heaven already knew it.

"Oh, sorry," Jane said trying to free a hand to hold out, then giving up on that. "Jane Anderson." She started to walk away, but Heaven followed along like she'd just found a new best friend.

"Do you work here?" Heaven asked, knowing that answer as well.

"No. Oh, I do work for Foster's, but my office is actually downtown, not here at the plant," Jane answered, narrowing her eyes at Heaven. "Are you a reporter?"

That took Heaven by surprise. "No. I just said I was a chef . . . but I suppose a reporter could lie about their profession. Haven't you ever been to Café Heaven on Thirty-ninth Street? Well, you wouldn't necessarily recognize me even if you'd eaten at my place. I'm usually in the kitchen. Why did you think I was a reporter, because of the problem last week?"

Jane laughed a bitter little laugh. "What a dainty way to put it, the 'problem' last week." She walked on silently.

"What do you do for Foster's?" Heaven asked, keeping pace. She knew she was being a pain in the ass, but she had to get a couple of answers from someone on this fishing trip.

"I'm the graphic designer. One of them anyway." Jane bit her lip. Why couldn't she just say she headed the graphics department, why couldn't she take credit?

Heaven remembered hearing something about the graphics department of Foster's. Where had that come up in the last week? "I bet you've had lots of design work what with all this new, what's it called, second-tier production?"

They were almost at the entrance of the plant. Jane stopped walking and turned toward Heaven. "It's been a real challenge, that's for sure."

Heaven touched Jane's arm lightly. She decided she had nothing to lose in offending this woman and information to gain. "Please explain something to me. When you were ill last Sunday, on the stage. Why did you stop in front of that other woman and accuse her of doing something to make you sick? Do body builders play dirty?"

Jane stiffened. "Not that it's any of your business, but

I'd had a problem with that particular contestant and I thought she was trying to get even for something . . . something she thought I'd done to her. Now I think I was paranoid. Are you coming in?"

Heaven smiled sweetly. "I apologize. I know it's none of my business as you said, but it did happen publicly, and I just wondered about it. I'm new to this body building world. And no, I've already been in to visit with Harold, poor man. I guess you know what happened?"

"No, what are you talking about?" Now Jane spoke roughly.

Oh well, she would have found out as soon as she went inside. "One of your employers, Claude Foster, was arrested just a little bit ago, for the murder of Oliver Bodden."

Jane almost dropped her papers. "Oh my God, Uncle Claude," she gasped and ran inside.

So that's where Heaven had heard about the graphic designer for Foster's, from Stephanie. This was cousin Janie.

Stephanie sat down and pushed her hair back, managing to get chocolate all over her forehead in the process. She was a mess, disheveled and spotted with chocolate, certainly not like her usual turned-out self. The store was packed with customers and Stephanie and her staff couldn't seem to keep up with the demand for fancy chocolates. "You've got to be kidding. That's as crazy as arresting *me* for that guy's murder. After all, I was the one standing there with the murder weapon in my hand."

Heaven decided to let that one pass by without mentioning how lucky Stephanie was she hadn't been hauled downtown in handcuffs. "And then," Heaven said as she tossed popcorn in a big bowl with melted chocolate, "I got to meet your cousin." Chocolate popcorn was a Chocolate Queen bestseller.

"Weird, isn't she?"

"She didn't do anything weird today, but as it turns out, I've seen Jane Anderson two other times in the last couple of weeks. And she was plenty weird."

Stephanie went over to a row of Granny Smith apples that had already been dipped in chocolate and started drizzling caramel on them. "Tell me," she said, not having the strength to ask more specific questions.

"I went with Joe to see a friend of his in a body building contest at Woodside and someone accused Joe's friend of being a man, not a woman. She was dykey, but obviously a female, to me at least. I guess in the body builder world, if someone questions, you have to go and have a gender test and it's humiliating. It was your cousin doing the accusing."

Stephanie clucked. "How rude."

"Then, the finals of this body building season, or whatever they have, were Sunday over at the old Seville Square. Your cousin, only I didn't know it was your cousin, had a spell on stage and had to drop out. She blamed Joe's friend and made quite a scene."

"What kind of spell?"

"She kind of collapsed. Sweat was pouring down her face and apparently she puked. I didn't see her, but the nurse told me. The nurse also told me that it occurs fairly often at these contests, that the contestants don't eat and then take megavitamins and they're stressed out and their stomachs can't hack it."

"And Janie blamed Joe's friend for all this?"

"On Sunday, but today she said it was probably something she ate. She's a strange one, you were right about that. Steph, do you think you should tell your mother about your uncle, so she doesn't see it on the evening news? Even with all the bad blood, I'm sure it will upset her."

Stephanie quickly went over and started washing her hands. "Thank God you still have your wits about you. I'm so tired I just can't think. I've got to warn Mom and Uncle David. He's working the floor." She quickly dis- sappeared out to the selling floor. In a minute she came back holding the hand of a minute version of the other two Foster brothers. David had his brother Harold's thick, wavy hair and his handsome face, but he was only about five foot eight. He was nattily dressed in college professor clothes: tweed jacket, crewneck sweater and Dockers. "Heaven, here's my uncle David. As you know I've put him to work. David, Heaven just came from the Foster's factory and guess what? Uncle Claude has been arrested for murdering that Oliver Bodden I told you about."

David Foster grinned. Heaven was a little surprised he didn't even try to hide his amusement at the situation. He held out his hand and shook Heaven's. "It couldn't happen to a more deserving person. Glad to meet you, Heaven. Sorry I'm not exhibiting the approriate amount of concern for my brother. After all he's done for me."

Heaven felt the hairs on the back of her neck stand up. This guy had issues. "I'm glad to meet you. I was telling Steph that someone should probably call her mother, before it appears on the six o'clock news."

David nodded. "I'll take care of that if you want me to, Steph. And I'll call my other sis and try not to crow," he said as he moved to the phone on the desk.

Stephanie looked at her friend with a helpless expression.

"I'm glad it was him and not you," Heaven said and patted her friend on the behind. "The popcorn is all mixed up but I can't stay and bag it. I've got to go to work. My baby girl is coming home tonight with her elderly boyfriend. Do you want to come have dinner with us?"

"I have to stay here until nine, and I can't imagine I'll be good company after that. But I'm looking forward to Christmas Eve."

"Remember, the first Christmas in retail on the Plaza is the hardest."

Stephanie gave a weak smile. "And just in case it wasn't hard enough, the fates have added a little family scandal. Heaven, I forgot to ask. Surely Claude wasn't charged with the blimp shooting too, was he?"

"No, I think that one is still up for grabs," Heaven said as she went out the side door with a handful of chocolate popcorn.

Heaven hurried into the kitchen. "Sorry I'm late. Has anything terrible happened?"

Jumpin' Jack turned from the work table and smiled at Heaven. "Your daughter called. She said they were stuck at JFK and they won't be in at six as scheduled. She'll call as they're getting on the plane. She said Stuart had ordered a car for them so they'd come right to the restaurant to meet you for dinner."

"Oh, okay," Heaven said, disappointment flooding her system. She hated the part about Stuart hiring a car, but she supposed it was better than waiting at the airport for hours. Now a hired driver could do the waiting. "What are you working on, Jack?"

Jack had been employed in the kitchen for only a few months. Before that he had been a local 39th Street character who dressed only in camo, thought he'd been to Vietnam but hadn't and helped Heaven with her sleuthing occasionally. Then he went a little too crazy and went to Menninger's, the famous mental hospital in Topeka, Kansas, gave up the camo and asked for a real job at the restaurant when he got out of the hospital. Jack hadn't ever needed a job because his rich parents paid him to stay out of their hair. The shrinks suggested, however, that earning his own way might be a good thing, self-esteem-wise. It seemed to be working.

"I just made the salad dressing for the Blu Heaven and now I'm going to fry the pecans. I'm doing salads tonight," he said proudly.

"Good man. Did the rabbits come in?"

Jack moved quickly to the walk-in and brought out a plastic container. "Here they are. What are you doing with them?"

Heaven went over to the bulletin board by the kitchen door and squinted at a recipe. "It's an Italian hunter's sauce kind of thing, without the blood, which is an ingredient in classic hunter's sauces. Mine has red wine and herbs and some chocolate at the end. That's why I was attracted to the dish, because of the chocolate. I prepared it last year in the winter and it's very good."

"Heaven," Murray Steinblatz yelled from the dining room. "Your friend Dale is here."

"That was quick," Heaven muttered. "At least I got to spend ten minutes in the kitchen." She took off the apron she had just put on and slipped on a 1950s sharkskin men's jacket that she kept in the kitchen on a coat hanger.

Dale Traver was drinking coffee with Murray, standing by the bar at Murray's spot. The two men laughed at something Murray said as Heaven crossed the dining room, walking into a shaft of sunlight coming in the front windows. She loved this time of day. It was that twilight zone for restaurants, the time between lunch and dinner service when things slowed down slightly. The only other person in the room was a wholesale liquor delivery man, bringing in wine. Murray was checking in the order as he talked.

Heaven gave Dale the two-cheek air kiss. "How's my favorite sleuth?" Dale asked.

"Full of news. You probably don't know this yet, but Claude Foster was arrested this morning for the murder, well, manslaughter, of Oliver Bodden, Friday's victim."

"They don't think he shot down his own airship, do they?"

"No, I don't think that was part of the charges."

He cocked his head at Heaven. "Well, Heaven, you were so right about my photographer Santa. I think I've talked to everyone in the building now, everyone who hasn't left yet for Palm Springs or Arizona. No one hired a Santa photographer for their Christmas party that Sunday, or any kind of Santa, for that matter. I was most likely polite to the airship sniper. I was almost in the same elevator with him," Dale said with excitement in his voice.

"We don't know that for sure. But with what you found out, and I can't thank you enough for that, it does look like the Santa could be the bad guy."

Dale took Heaven's hand. "It was my pleasure, I assure you. I've never known so much about my building and its occupants. I've got to go. Have a good holiday."

"Wait. I want you come to my house on Christmas Eve, if you're not busy with family."

"No, I'm not having dinner with my niece and her family out in Overland Park until Christmas Day."

"Come down any time after seven." Heaven grabbed a restaurant business card and scribbled on it. "Here's my address. You must see Iris all grown up now. She's home from England, or will be in a few hours."

"I can hardly wait. I'll bring champagne," Dale said and he left with a cheery wave.

Heaven was excited. Her hunch about the Santa was right, she just knew it was. Not that it did them much good, since Bonnie wouldn't call her back. Besides, identifying a Santa on the Plaza that particular day would be like finding a needle in a haystack. She hurried back to the kitchen to fix the rabbit.

Heaven was pacing. She said she was working the room, but really she was pacing. Because of Iris's arrival tonight, Heaven had replaced herself in the kitchen, and now it was seven and Iris wasn't here and all she could do was pace. Oh, she talked to every table, wished them a happy holiday season, but she was wound up and the whole staff was avoiding her as much as possible.

"Heaven, why don't you have a nice glass of wine," Murray said, like he was talking to a small child and offering chocolate milk.

"When did she say they got in?" Heaven asked, for the tenth time.

"Six forty-six. But even with a limo waiting for them, it's going to be another half hour. So, what would you like?"

"I didn't see that four top in the back. That's Eric, our dried herb and spice guy and his wife. I'll just pop back and say hi," Heaven said and took off for the back of the room.

Murray sighed. Just then, Bonnie Weber came charging through the door. "I need a beer," she bellowed.

Tony, behind the bar, pointed at her. "Boulevard pale ale, right?"

"I'd drink anything with a little kick to it right now. In fact, Tony, change that to a Stoli martini straight up with a twist."

She plopped down on the bar stool nearest Murray. "Where's the Queen of Thirty-ninth Street?"

"She's jumping out of her skin, waiting for her daughter."

"Iris is coming home for Christmas? That must be making Heaven happy."

"Yes, except she's bringing her boyfriend, Stuart Watts," Murray said under his breath, not wanting Heaven to catch them talking about Stuart.

Bonnie accepted her drink from Tony and held it up in salute to Murray, then took a sip. "Ah, yes, this was a better idea than beer. I didn't know that Iris was involved with Watts." She used the musician's last name like she was talking about a suspect. "Isn't he in her father's band?"

"Yes, and that's what's bothering Heaven. She thinks he's too old and she knows him too well."

Before Bonnie could ask another question, Heaven swirled up beside her. "Oh, my God. I thought you'd abandoned me. How dare you make an arrest without telling me first?"

Bonnie looked at Murray. "She is a little high-strung tonight, isn't she?"

Murray hurried off to seat a deuce that had just arrived, hoping Heaven wouldn't explode.

She didn't. In fact, she was so glad to see Bonnie she didn't even yell at her about not returning the phone calls. "So, what made you arrest Claude?" she asked even before she ordered a drink. "Tony, may I have a glass of Cloudy Bay Sauvignon Blanc?"

"No martini?" Bonnie challenged.

"No, I have to stay fairly sober tonight, so I don't go off on Iris's boyfriend."

"I want to hear about that," Bonnie said. "After we discuss my superior criminalist work. I guess we always knew Claude had the motive, or at least we knew that once we started looking into the business practices at Foster's. Oliver Bodden was a partner who was somehow squeezing the brothers. I do know they've been trying to finance a buyout of the West African Cacao Company, going around to local banks. And you weren't the only one to hear Claude talking bad about the Bodden fellow. Everyone in the plant had seen or heard something. You also weren't the only one to see brother Claude leave the press show, although I must tell you I'm pissed that I missed that myself. I'm sure he thought his speeches would give him an alibi. So he has opportunity, he certainly has the motive if this guy is trying to steal the business, and the means, those packing wires, were piled in a big box not three feet from where the victim was found. And his fingerprints were found all over the conch machine."

"But think about the guy's physical appearance, Bonnie. He's a ninety-eight-pound weakling. Do you really think he could choke Oliver Bodden with a wire hard enough to cut off his air? Come on."

"I think he found Oliver, they had words and Oliver

turned his back on Claude—maybe he was leaning over checking the conch gadget. Claude was mad in the first place and having this dude be so unconcerned just took him over the top. He probably beaned him with something, he fell in the conching gizmo, Claude grabbed a metal wire from the shipping area and showed Oliver who was still boss at Foster's. When you're angry, you have that adrenaline strength. Or, Claude and he fought, Claude strangled him, then heard the group coming his way and shoved Bodden in the conch machine because he did know he wouldn't be able to lug the big guy out of there successfully. Claude will tell us how it went down soon, I'm sure. I'm meeting with him and his attorney tomorrow. Regular joes like him always end up confessing. Speaking of confessing, now is the perfect time for you to tell me what you were doing at Foster's today."

Heaven ignored that. "What I don't understand is the fire of all the cocoa beans. What's that about?"

"That's when I knew I had a case, my dear. I talked to the guys on the factory floor. Now, they seem to really like their bosses, the Fosters. It wasn't like everyone was eager to see them go down. But I just played dumb, which I am about chocolate production, and certain facts came out. Here's what I think happened. No one from the factory was around when the fire happened so I'm flying by the seat of my pants."

"The secretary today told me that thousands of dollars of cocoa beans were burned and the brothers said it must be vandalism, but she wasn't buying it," Heaven added.

"Do you want to hear or not?" Bonnie asked impatiently. "No one went for the vandalism excuse. For one thing, the only cocoa beans that weren't burned were the ones from West African Cacao. Then, the foreman explained this whole nibs thing to me. The good chocolate companies have a secret blend of cocoa beans from all over the world, actually the nibs are the inside of the bean, that's what they blend. A company will use up to twelve different kinds of nibs."

"I knew that," Heaven said, remembering her chocolate lecture from Stephanie.

"Except Foster's was only using West African nibs in the new chocolate. They weren't blending a thing. The foreman thought it was some kind of a strong-arm tactic on the part of Bodden, said it would ruin the taste of the chocolate. I examined the burned bags, at least a few I found in the back of the Dumpster. They were from Mexico and Costa Rica. I think Oliver Bodden burned up the beans from other countries to make a point."

Heaven hugged Bonnie's arm. "Good investigating, girlfriend. But I just want to tell you that I met the other brother, David, today at the Chocolate Queen and when I told him about Claude he was estactic—well, happy at least. It was very creepy. I think he could do anything to get even with his brothers for the old doublecross. I haven't been able to get him out if my mind."

Bonnie shrugged. "I'll at least check with the airlines to see when he arrived in Kansas City. I'd love if he was a sharpshooter and secretly arrived weeks ago. I'd love to tie both of the Foster crimes up in a nice, tidy bundle. I can't see Claude for the airship incident, can you?"

"Why would he? Oh, look, here's my darling daughter," Heaven practically squealed. She swooped toward the door and grabbed Iris in a bear hug. Behind her Stuart Watts stood tall in the doorway. His dark hair was spiked with gray, but he was still a handsome figure.

"Hi, Mom. Can we ride home with you? I told Stuart it was silly to have the driver wait."

"Of course, honey. Just have the driver bring your bags in. We'll stick them in the office."

Iris went over to hug Murray and say hello to Bonnie, so Heaven turned to face Stuart. "Welcome to Kansas City," she said.

Stuart bowed and took Heaven's hand, kissed it and smiled up at her. "Heaven, I know you're not thrilled about this, about Iris and me."

"Stop it," Heaven ordered, giving herself an internal warning about her tone of voice. "I'm just glad to have Iris home. Happy Holidays, Stuart." She took his hand and led him to the bar. "Tony, get this man a drink."

Chocolate Empanadas

8 oz. good chocolate (I used semisweet but milk chocolate would be good too.)

¼ to ⅓ cup cajeta, the Mexican caramel, or other good caramel sauce

⅓ cup toasted nuts

⅓ cup dried fruit

Frozen Asian dumpling wrappers, defrosted

Canola oil for frying

¼ tsp. cinnamon

For dusting: approx. 1 cup of confectioners' sugar sifted over the hot empanadas or combine 1 cup sugar with 1 tsp. cinnamon to dredge the fried empanadas in.

Finely chop the chocolate and mix with the other ingredients. I used two terrific combinations: almonds and golden raisins, and pine nuts and dates. You could also use combinations such as dried cranberries or cherries and pecans or dried apricots and hazelnuts.

To fill, dip a finger in a small bowl of water, and wet the edges of the dumpling wrapper. Try not to get the middle of the wrapper wet so it will not crack open. Put a spoonful of chocolate filling in the wrapper and close the edges with your wet finger, pinching shut firmly. This amount of filling will make 40–50 empanadas.

After forming the empanadas, let set at least an hour or refrigerate overnight. Fry in an inch or so of medium hot oil. The wrappers will brown in about a minute and a half per side. Drain and dust with confectioners' sugar or a mixture of sugar and cinnamon. These are great for a buffet. If you want to use them at a sit-down party, garnish the plate with warm cajeta sauce and some berries or diced mango and the toasted nut used in the filling.

Nine

"I can't carry another package," Iris gasped.

Heaven smiled. "I'm so glad we did this. I hadn't done much Christmas shopping. What a good idea you had, to get Hank a tuxedo."

"Mom, he'll look like a movie star in it. And doctors do need to dress up occasionally, I would think, especially if they live with the famous Heaven Lee. I need an espresso." Iris was almost whining.

"You're right about the first part. He'll be gorgeous in his new Armani tux. But the famous Heaven Lee part is hooey," Heaven said with a big smile on her face, obviously complimented. "Let's go around the corner to Stephanie's for a coffee drink and some chocolate." She guided her daughter around a busy corner on the Plaza.

Today was special for Heaven. Christmas shopping with her daughter was the kind of activity she had missed so much in the last few years after Iris had gone off to England for college. As she spotted her own image reflected in a store window she realized she was positively beaming and almost skipping along beside her daughter. She blushed, embarrassed at her own happiness, and tried to look more sedate.

When the two women opened the door of the Chocolate Queen, Stephanie Simpson slammed down a telephone behind the counter. "Where have you been? I've been trying to call you every ten minutes for an hour."

"And a cheery hello to you too," Heaven said.

"Hi, Iris," Stephanie said distractedly. "Come in the back."

Iris looked longingly at the espresso machine.

"Get a latte and a treat, then come in the back," Heaven said, getting Iris off the hook.

The store was crowded and Stephanie didn't say anything until they were down in the basement, a rather dungeon-like place with stone walls and uneven concrete floors. She quickly sent the two employees that were taking a break down there back up to the selling floor, then flung herself in a chair. "Do you remember about two years ago when the couple that owned the bin candy stores got in trouble?"

Heaven frowned. "Vaguely. Was it something about bugs in their candy?"

"Yes, and Stan Kramer did an exposé on Channel Five and—"

Heaven broke in. "Now I remember. There were creepy shots of bugs in those plastic bins. Ugh."

Stephanie nodded, not looking up at Heaven, her head in her hands. "Yes, and then they went out of business. Broke. Bankrupt."

"I sure didn't want to eat any gummy bears out of those bins after that."

"Well, I'm ruined," Stephanie said dramatically.

Heaven was beginning to be irritated. "Your store is

full of affluent Christmas shoppers buying things. Why are we talking about the bin candy people and how can you be ruined?"

Stephanie went over to a work counter and pulled a large plastic storage container out from under, sitting it on top of the counter with a flourish. "Open it if you dare."

Heaven jerked the lid off. The container was full of ten-pound blocks of chocolate. And the chocolate was moving. She peered in the container more closely and realized there were some sort of white worms winding in and out of the chocolate. Lots of them. She closed the top and snapped it shut tightly. "Is it just one tub?"

"I wish," Stephanie said. "There were four of those and I've already thrown away the other three, tub and all. I kept this one to show you and maybe Bonnie Weber."

"Bonnie? I know it's upsetting but it's not exactly a crime. It's not as bad as stuff I've seen in my own restaurant kitchen. Things grow. One fly is left in the whole universe and it finds its way to food and then there are maggots."

"I do not have maggots," Stephanie said, practically screaming.

"Look, I think I'm missing something here. And keep your voice down, for God's sake. The word 'maggot' shouldn't be yelled out in a place that sells food. Whatever the little critters are. Aside from the obvious cost connected with all the chocolate you had to pitch today, no candy you're selling on the floor was affected, was it?"

"No, but I haven't checked every single piece of candy. And it will only take one to finish me," Stephanie said, refusing to give up her position that ruin was around the corner.

"So be sure and give your employees a good talking to about keeping the lids on these containers sealed at all times."

"Heaven, we always keep the lids on. Someone came in here and put bugs in my chocolate. That's the only explanation."

Heaven immediately thought about Uncle David. "Are these blocks kept down here in the basement?"

"No, in the room upstairs by the selling floor. And I'm sure this chocolate was just fine yesterday. I know it has to do with all these Foster's problems, I just know it," Stephanie said with feeling.

"You may be right," a male voice said from the top of the stairs.

"Mom, what's going on?" Iris called down.

Together Iris and Uncle David came down the stairs. "This is Stephanie's uncle, David," Iris said. "We met upstairs."

"Yes, we met the other day. David, why did you say you may be right?" Heaven asked, knowing she was slightly rude. Her instincts about this guy were telling her he could sabatoge Stephanie too.

"Because Stephanie may be right. This may be connected to the Foster's candy drama." He turned to Stephanie. "I was visiting your mom before I came to work and your aunt called. It seems Janie called home and there's been a whole batch of chocolate, hundreds of pounds, that suddenly has bloom on it. And the foreman is sure it was fine a couple of days ago."

Iris held up her hand. "Okay. What's bloom?"

Heaven knew Stephanie would give a lengthy lecture on bloom so she answered quickly before Stephanie could. "I don't know all the chemistry but air and moisture combine somehow and the surface of the chocolate becomes discolored, lighter than it should be."

"That icky white stuff?" Iris said, wrinkling her nose.

"It doesn't really hurt the chocolate but it does render it unsalable," David said and then smiled at Heaven and his niece. "Just because I didn't get to work in the company doesn't mean I don't know about chocolate. It seems someone doesn't want any of the Fosters in the candy business to have a good Christmas."

Heaven was sure he had a look of satisfaction on his face as he talked about his family's problems. They needed another nutty Foster family member like they needed another hole in the head. "That's it. I'm calling Bonnie," she announced and no one argued.

Everyone was talking at once.

Bonnie had agreed to meet Heaven and whoever else she wanted to bring along at Heaven's favorite Mexican restaurant down on Southwest Boulevard, the Hispanic section of Kansas City. Heaven had insisted Stephanie and David come along and Iris had called Stuart to meet them. Hank came from the hospital only thirty minutes late. Now they had a long table full of food, two pitchers of margaritas, and plenty of opinions. The days' discoveries, bloom on the chocolate at Foster's and bugs at the Chocolate Queen, met with mixed reviews from the crowd. Some found it more significant than others did.

Hank took a logical approach. "Both of these things could have occurred naturally. I know it's a weird coincidence, but the discoloration, the larvae, both could be the product of simple accidents."

Bonnie nodded. "Hank's right. Carelessness on the

part of workers could have caused both of them, and I'd be inclined to believe that was the case if there wasn't the tiny little problem of a sniper taking down the Foster's airship and killing its pilot, then Oliver Bodden's murder. When you add them all up, it stinks."

David Foster turned toward the detective. "But I thought you'd arrested my brother for the Oliver Bodden death. He's still in jail, isn't he?"

"No, as a matter of fact, he's not," Bonnie said. "He posted bail. That's the American justice system, you know. Unless the accused is a flight risk bail must be set. And the judge and even the prosecutor didn't believe your uncle was going to fly the coop. Strong ties to the community, they call it."

Stephanie held up her hand dramatically. "This doesn't make sense. Not that I believe Uncle Claude killed that man I found in the conching machine, but even if he had an argument with the victim and somehow things got out of hand and he *did* kill him by accident, Uncle Claude would have no reason to ruin a big batch of his own chocolate or shoot down the anniversary blimp."

"If he wouldn't trash his own product, how about yours?" Heaven asked.

"It still doesn't make sense," Stephanie said again. "I've been open for months and I've lived in this town my whole life. Why would Claude wait until he was under indictment for murder to start harassing me? The man's not stupid."

"He's not moral, either," David mentioned quite caustically.

Heaven's ears perked up from her chair on the other side of David. Even if Stephanie's mother and aunt didn't hold a grudge, it sure sounded like Uncle David did. "I have news, Bonnie," Heaven announced.

"I bet you do," Bonnie said with a weary sigh. This case was getting out of hand.

"I went to visit a friend of mine who lives in that tall condo behind Barnes and Noble on the Plaza. I was hoping he'd been home on the Sunday of the airship attack and might have seen someone up on the roof. He lives in the penthouse."

"Gosh, Heaven, what a good idea. Why didn't I think of that the day of the attack? Oh, wait a minute, I did think of it," Bonnie said, pouring herself another margarita.

"I know you sent uniforms around but they didn't talk to my friend because he wasn't home. He went to the Nutcracker Ballet. But as he was leaving the building, there was a Santa Claus with cameras and a camera case waiting for the elevator. He thought the Santa was going to work a children's party but then later he asked everyone in the building and no one hired a Santa that day, so I'm pretty sure it was the sniper. Those metal Halliburton camera cases could carry a gun," Heaven said.

"You've involved another civilian in investigative work, haven't you," Bonnie said accusingly. "He didn't ask his fellow apartment dwellers until you told him to."

Heaven waved her hand impatiently. "Dale, my friend Dale Traver, has a natural in, living there. His neighbors were probably much more forthcoming with him than they would be with your people, the uniforms."

A server arrived with a platter of flaky fried pockets of dough dripping with *cajeta* caramel sauce.

"What are those?" Iris asked.

"Chocolate-filled empanadas," Heaven said, grabbing one. "It's a house specialty."

Bonnie took an empanada and pulled a legal pad out

of her large tote bag and slammed it down in front of Heaven. "Now they're 'my people,' eh? Bull. Write down his name and phone number. I'll talk to this guy, one of your people. Is there any other little side investigation you're doing that I should know about?"

Heaven thought about cousin Janie, but decided to keep her mouth shut. That really fell under the body building mysteries area anyway.

Stuart Watts, who found himself in the strange position of not being the center of attention, had been rather enjoying this state of affairs. He'd always gotten a kick out of Heaven and she had definitely not mellowed with age, that was obvious. He reached across the table and touched Iris's hand. She was talking to Stephanie about lipstick colors. What a dear. He decided to weigh in on this chocolate matter. "Chocolate has an interesting history," Stuart said. "The Spanish found it in Mexico and it had been used for years down there. The Dutch improved it and then of course the Brits, and others, too, exploited it to the hilt."

"What do you mean by that?" Iris asked.

"Took it to Africa where they've turned it into a big business in the Ivory Coast and other parts of West Africa. But there's a problem, just like with the other bloody crops that Europeans took a liking to."

"Like coffee and tea?" Heaven offered.

"Exactly," Stuart said. "We learn to love this stuff that takes the exploitation of workers to produce. Usually it grows best in nasty equatorial weather, people make little or nothing for working with it. Like the slaves who worked the cotton and sugarcane down in your South."

"Surely chocolate has nothing to do with slaves?" Stephanie said, uncomfortable at the thought.

"Yes, it absolutely has to do with slaves. They did a big

send-up in one of the London papers just a few months ago. Little boys were sold by their own parents to these middlemen who sold them to plantation owners in the Ivory Coast. Kept them locked up in bloody pens. Didn't pay them a dime and beat them as well. Makes the old hot fudge sundae rather pricey, don't you think, in terms of human sacrifice?"

The table fell silent. No one had thought about their chocolate in quite those terms before. Heaven was really irritated that a rock star richer than God was discussing the fate of equatorial workers. He could pay all the chocolate workers out of his own pocket if it really bothered him so much. The slave-labor angle was intriguing, though, she had to admit. "Bonnie, what if the thugs and Oliver Bodden were part of a slave labor ring and somehow the brothers had found out about it and were going to expose them? No, that doesn't get Claude off the hook, does it. What if Oliver was going to blow the whistle on the slave labor ring back home and the thugs killed him because of that?"

For some reason, maybe the margaritas, everyone at the table thought this was a great idea. Perhaps the idea of evil slave lords from Africa was easier to take than Uncle Claude putting a packing wire around Oliver Bodden's neck. It was Bonnie who brought the group back down to earth.

"So the slave lords from Africa shot down an airship, killed Oliver Bodden and then started playing dirty tricks on all the chocolate in Kansas City? Busy, aren't they?" Bonnie said as she stood up and threw down two twenties on the table. "Slave labor is an awful appetite depressant, that's for sure. But I don't think it's at the bottom of our problems here in Kansas City. Everything revolves around the Foster family and so I'm going to get busy on the phone and insist that everyone who's in that family and in this town come to Café Heaven tomorrow morning at ten for a little sit down."

"Why Café Heaven?" Stephanie asked.

"Would you rather come down to police headquarters? Or have all of us come to Heaven's place of business?" Bonnie asked.

"Café Heaven sounds good," Stephanie said.

Heaven was thrilled, of course. But she knew Bonnie would give her a lecture of some kind. She was right.

"Café Heaven is convenient for this meeting because it will not be open at ten in the morning and the chef/owner will be busy in the kitchen and not sticking her nose in my business. Got it?" Bonnie barked, looking hard at Heaven. "Thanks for a lovely evening," she said as she walked out.

When you got them all together there were lots of Fosters. Uncle David. Stephanie and her mom and dad. Cousin Janie and her mom and dad, the Andersons. Junior and his wife, though none of their daughters were in attendance because they weren't coming home for the holidays this year. Claude was by himself. His wife hadn't been out of bed since he was arrested, having always been prone to sick headaches. No one mentioned Claude's son but Heaven remembered hearing that he didn't live in Kansas City. Stephanie's grandmother was there, looking worried but also obviously happy to see her children together again.

Heaven was peeking out at this gathering in the dining room from the kitchen side of the pass-through window. She'd set out two carafes of coffee, one with caffeine, one without. She'd also gone to Lamar's doughnuts on her way in to work and picked up several dozen of the local favorite, left a dozen glazed in the kitchen for the crew, and put the rest out for the family.

"Things will go so much better if everyone gets revved up on coffee and sugar," Bonnie said when she saw the spread. Bonnie had arrived early and reminded Heaven that she didn't want to see her snooping around.

"I know you'll be using your waitress ears to try to hear, but I don't want to see even the top of your red head, do you understand?" Bonnie said sternly.

Heaven didn't really know what Bonnie was thinking would happen at this family reunion. "I'll stay out of the way, but I don't get it. What do you hope to gain by this?"

"I'm losing control. I never had control but every day some new piece of crap happens and it all revolves around this family, a family that doesn't even speak to each other and hasn't for years. I wanted to see if they would meet together and then I want them to understand that even though I arrested Claude for the murder of Oliver Bodden, and I think he's the perp, there is still something dangerous going on. Now leave me alone," Bonnie'd ordered and she'd paced around the dining room until the Fosters straggled in. By ten everyone was present and accounted for, punctuality being a desirable Kansas City trait.

"Don't think this is going to be like one of those meetings at the end of *Murder She Wrote*, where Jessica has it all figured out," Bonnie said to the group. "This is more of a warning than anything."

"Warning of what?" Claude said suspiciously.

"I want you all to be on the alert. I think someone is seriously trying to destroy your family," she said with as much gravity as she could muster. "And I can't seem to protect you."

Claude stood up, his thin body quivering with rage. "Protect us? You've accused and arrested me for murder. You're the one who's ruining our family business. You're destroying us."

Brother David snorted. "She can't ruin my family business because I don't have a family business. My brothers stole my share of it away from me a long time ago."

With that, the grandmother started to cry, Stephanie's mom went down to the end of the table to comfort her and everyone started to yell at everyone else. Bonnie let it go for a couple of minutes, then she whistled her ballpark whistle and yelled, "Shut up!" at the top of her lungs. "This is a real problem, folks. I want you all to be aware of what's happened here. First, someone who knew their way around a rifle shot down the Foster's anniversary blimp and killed the pilot."

As some of the crowd started to speak, Bonnie whistled again. "I said shut up. Now what I've found out about the pilot leads me to believe he was collateral damage, that his death wasn't the primary goal of that attack, that if his death was planned, it was planned in relation to him being the pilot of the airship you, the part of the Foster family that owns the chocolate company," she said, staring hard at Uncle David as if daring him to pipe up again, then turning back toward Junior, "hired to celebrate your company's anniversary. From what I've learned about your family rift, there are probably people in this very room who would have been happy to chip in on some kind of unhappy accident for that airship, if not for the death of an innocent man. If any of you have anything to tell me in that regard, know that I understand how these things turn bad. On paper, maybe someone in this room thought no one could get hurt, that all it would do was cause trouble for the brothers who I'm sure some of you think deserve trouble. Then something went wrong and the pilot was killed. If this is the case, please call me and I'll go with you to the prosecutor's office, explain some of the back history. I will help you if you come to me."

Heaven peeked out and saw Stephanie's mother return to her seat, lean over to her husband and pat his hand. Stephanie had kept her eyes lowered through most of Bonnie's speech. Now she was looking down the table at her grandmother. Heaven could see tears in both of their eyes.

Heaven wondered about that hand pat. Surely Stephanie's father hadn't gone berserk and shot down that airship. No, it couldn't be him, the kindly general practitioner. Stephanie said her mother didn't even allow guns in the house. Heaven went over and checked some squash she was baking in the oven. But maybe he had a gun at the office. Maybe he had been harboring resentment all these years. Heaven rolled her neck around, trying to rid her head of paranoid thinking. No way. It was just a hand pat. She went back over to the window.

The whole group looked so unhappy and here they were together for the first time in years. What a waste. Business and families could be such a terrible combination.

Bonnie continued. "I wish I thought the whole airship mess was just a vindictive prank gone wrong. And we won't talk about the death of Oliver Bodden because it is an active investigation involving one of you. With the things that happened yesterday, I'm afraid we have a nut on our hands who is angry at the whole Foster family, and that worries me. If we eliminate the death of Oliver

143

Bodden from the equation, we still have quite enough coincidences to make me nervous."

"What happened yesterday?" Stephanie's grandmother asked.

Bonnie held up her hand like a sidewalk crossing guard to indicate she was going to answer and everyone else should be quiet. "Chocolate was sabotaged at both the Chocolate Queen and the Foster's factory. Now that Stephanie's business has also had a problem, I have strong gut feelings that there is a person out there who is very angry at the Foster family, or one of you who is very angry at the rest of you."

A clamor of noise broke loose again. Stephanie stood up. "But what about the information that came out last night? What if all of this has something to do with child slave labor at the cacao plantations in Africa? What if it doesn't have anything to do with the Fosters, except as we are chocolate candymakers?"

You could tell by the looks on their faces that the child slavery issue wasn't something Junior and Claude were up on. They looked horrified, as if they needed another negative thing concerning their business right now. Heaven, peeking out the pass-through window, couldn't imagine what it would be like to find out that a product that your whole business was based on used slave labor.

She had been thinking about it from her restaurant's perspective overnight. If chocolate wasn't such a popular product, she might eliminate it from her menus. But as it was, even she, a liberal by anyone's definition of the term, couldn't imagine doing that. Stephanie, and certainly the brothers, didn't have a choice. It was their entire business.

Bonnie was trying to quiet everyone down again.

"Hold on, hold on. I would imagine that if a group were going to protest your businesses because of child labor practices in the chocolate industry, they would protest publicly and let people know why they were upset, especially because this isn't something that's widely talked about in the United States. It wouldn't bring any awareness of the problems in Africa if they nailed an airship in Kansas City and didn't come out and say why they did it, or if they killed Oliver Bodden, for that matter. I think this is someone who is watching silently right here in Kansas City and is enjoying every problem he or she has created for all of you. That's why I want to put you all on notice. You must be careful. You must be aware of what's going on around you. If even the slightest thing seems out of place, I want you to call me right away. I'm passing out my card with my cell phone and my home phone on it as well as my office. Now why don't you all just sit here together for a while and I'll get us some more coffee," Bonnie said, not asking but telling. She headed for the kitchen doors.

Heaven didn't even attempt to act like she hadn't been listening. She nodded at Bonnie as she came through the doors. "Good job."

"Then why don't I feel better?" Bonnie asked, holding up the coffee pot expectantly.

Heaven pointed back in the dining room. "It's over in the back corner. I made you another pot."

As Bonnie turned to go, Heaven thought of something. She put her hand on the detective's arm to get her attention. "Ask them to think back. If there was anyone they've recently fired or who had quit under negative circumstances, maybe they could put together a list of names. It could be a disgruntled employee."

Bonnie grinned. "Yes sir, Miss Heaven. I be askin'

them," she said as she pushed open the dining room door.

Marie Whitmer, secretary to Claude and Harold Foster, was nervous. She'd heard from Junior and he hadn't been very forthcoming, just said they had a meeting at ten and they would be in after that.

She speculated the meeting had been with Claude's lawyers. Everyone in the company was upset. They all came to her for information or for reassurance that everything would be straightened out and no one would lose their jobs. She, normally so on top of things, was at a loss as to what to tell them. And it was Christmas, a time when everyone wanted to spend money, enjoy their families. Instead, they were all scared to death they'd be out on the street, her included.

The phone rang and she grabbed it quickly, hoping it was the brothers. "Executive offices," she said by way of hello.

It wasn't the brothers. In fact, it wasn't anyone she wanted to talk to. "Oh, it's you. I told you not to call for a few days, that I'd call you," she said tersely.

The expression on her face was fearful. She always carried a cloth hankie and now she twisted it around her hand.

Mexican Mole Sauce

4 dried ancho chilies, stemmed and seeded
5 dried pasilla chilies, stemmed and seeded
6 dried mulato chilies, stemmed and seeded
½ cup raisins
Water
1 onion, peeled and diced
4 garlic cloves, peeled and sliced
4 T. lard or canola oil
½ tsp. cinnamon
¼ tsp. black pepper
¼ tsp. anise
Dash cloves
1 tsp. kosher salt
½ cup sesame seeds
½ cup peanuts or almonds
1 tortilla, fried crispy and torn up
1 oz. unsweetened chocolate, chopped

Soak the chilies and raisins for 30 minutes in warm water.

In a dry saute pan, lightly toast the spices. Lightly toast the sesame seeds and nuts in the oven.

Saute the onion and garlic in the lard until soft.

In a food processor, blend the chilies, raisins, cooked onion and garlic, spices, nuts, tortilla, chocolate and seeds together. You may have to do this in two batches.

Taste the soaking liquid from the chilies and if it isn't bitter, add it to the ground mix in a large heavy pan. If it is too bitter throw it away. Altogether you will want to add water and soaking liquid (or just water) to equal about 6 cups of liquid. Blend and simmer over low heat for 45 minutes.

This sauce is great with roasted turkey, roasted pork and chicken. It will keep in the refrigerator for 10 days. It is better after the flavors marry at least overnight.

Ten

It was weird. Heaven had felt happy all day, not the usual little fleeting jolts of happiness that only last a few minutes.

Since it was Christmas Eve and also Sunday, the restaurant was closed and wouldn't open again until Tuesday evening. She and Iris had cooked and carried on together at home, getting ready for an onslaught of people for their annual Christmas Eve party.

Stuart had departed on Saturday evening for the West Coast. Hank had negotiated to have Sunday evening off and in return he would go in to work tomorrow afternoon for another doctor who had a family. Both of these things, Stuart gone and Hank home, were part of the reason that Heaven was so upbeat. Hank had acted as the fix-it man around the house, changing lightbulbs and organizing the bar. He let Heaven and Iris have their space but he always seemed to know when they needed his help, to reach a baking pan on the top shelf or to taste test the guacamole.

People had started arriving about an hour ago, at seven, and the room was getting full.

Almost every employee of Café Heaven was here, except for a few who had gone out of town.

There were lots of Hank's colleagues from the hospital, and some of his Vietnamese friends from the neighborhood.

Earlier in the day, Iris had called some of her high-school friends who still lived in Kansas City and several had shown up.

Bonnie and her whole family had just arrived. Stephanie had shown up early, right after her shop closed at five, saying if she went home first and came at the appropriate time she'd fall asleep and sleep through Christmas. She'd brought leftovers from the shop with her and put out a huge tray of various chocolate items. Stephanie had asked earlier in the day if her uncle David could come to the party and he and Dale Traver were talking in a corner. Heaven was glad to be able to keep an eye on David.

Even Sal was here. Mona Kirk had insisted that they come together and had told him she would make the ultimate sacrifice and go north of the river to pick him up as she knew he didn't like to drive in the dark. Even though no one openly talked about it, forty years of squinting to cut hair had taken a toll on Sal's eyesight.

Heaven had whipped up several versions of mole sauce over the last several days, soaking chilies and roasting and grinding spices together with almonds and Mexican chocolate. One sauce was a golden color, one a dark orange, and one the color of burnt sugar. In the state of Oaxaca, turkey with mole was the traditional holiday combination so today she and Iris had roasted a big turkey plus a pork roast. Her kitchen crew had made tamales in their spare time over the last couple of weeks, freezing them as they were steamed. Tonight they were serving tamales filled with sweet corn, others with pork, and a third version with raisins, nuts and cinnamon.

Iris had peeled and mashed avocados to make a big batch of guacamole. Heaven had soaked and cooked a big pot of black beans and she'd made some salsas, but she'd bought freshly fried tortilla chips from La Posada, a grocery and café down on Southwest Boulevard. She didn't want to fry them at home and have the place smell like grease. While she was there she'd picked up a case of religious candles in tall glasses with saints' pictures on them, and they now flickered on the big serving table that was covered with Mexican oilcloth printed with flowers and fruit all over it. It was a festive table.

"Come and get it," Heaven yelled as she put down a cactus salad. "I think that's everything."

"You've done it again," Hank said and he kissed her on the cheek.

"Well, it's a bit different than most of us will have tomorrow, dry turkey and soggy dressing," Bonnie said as she scooped up some guacamole with a chip. "The dry turkey is my specialty. My kids won't recognize this juicy meat right here."

"But you make a mean bacon, lettuce and tomato sandwich as I recall," Heaven said as she gave her friend a hug. "Dig in."

"Good tree," Dale Traver said.

"Hank got it. Oh, Bonnie, here's my friend from the condo on the Plaza. Just ask him about the Santa, go ahead," Heaven said.

Bonnie winked at Dale. "We're old friends. We spent the day together, yesterday, as ol' Dale went around his building with me, talking to all the neighbors. He's a good recruit for your team of volunteer investigators, I must admit."

"She told me to never help you again without calling her first," Dale said, his eyes glowing with the enjoyment of being in on something.

"Well, did you find anyone who had hired a Santa photographer?" Heaven said, confident of the answer.

"No," Bonnie said as she spooned some of the orange-colored mole over a big piece of dark turkey meat, then unwrapped a pork tamale. "And I tend to agree with you and Dale. That could be our shooter. Too bad we don't have a better description."

Dale ducked his head. "I'm so sorry. Everyone looks the same in a Santa suit. And I was in a hurry to get to the ballet in time so I really didn't pay attention. It just registered that it was a Santa with cameras. Now, of course, I know the camera around his neck was probably just a prop and the camera case had a gun in it."

Bonnie threw an arm around Dale. "That's more info than I had before, Dale ol' buddy. Come meet my family," she said and led the older man away.

"Nice tree," Sal said, unlit cigar in his mouth as usual.

"Better than last year," Mona remarked as they both took an empty plate and looked over the spread of food.

Heaven looked over at the beautiful tree. "Hank got it. It's the best tree I've had in years. Hank taught me to appreciate a good tree and not to feel guilty about it."

"I guess you're pretty happy to have your girl home," Sal muttered as he stabbed a chunk of pork roast.

"Ecstatic," Heaven said. "I've been corny beyond belief, having her here for the holidays, crying and laughing at all the wrong times. Are you going to your daughter's tomorrow?"

"Oh, yeah," Sal said, grumbling. "Christmas is a bunch of hooey but the grandkids like it."

Mona gave him an elbow. "I went in over at Sal's and there were about three hundred presents all wrapped and under the cutest little tree. For someone who says Christmas is hooey you went all out."

Sal blushed, the top of his almost bald head turning red. "Mona, put a lid on it. I'm gonna go sit down by Murray," he said as he shambled away.

"I wonder if Sal can eat with that cigar still in place," Heaven said as she felt her eyes fill up with tears.

Mona looked at her friend with concern. "What's the matter, honey?"

"Nothing. This is just what I was talking about. I'm happy. Iris and I had a wonderful time together today. It's great having her home. And here I am with a beautiful Christmas tree and my house full of friends. How did I get so lucky?"

"Don't worry," Murray said as he grabbed a plate and started filling it. "Something will happen soon that'll bring you back to the real world. Enjoy it while it lasts."

Murray's wife had been killed by a car full of teenagers as she walked across a street in New York City so Murray was talking from experience. Heaven hit him lightly on the arm with her fist. "Don't be a spoiler. I know it won't last long. Stuart Watts will be back on Friday," she said and they all laughed.

Luckily, Iris and Joe Long sidled up beside Heaven after she made the smart crack about Stuart so Iris didn't know her mother was getting laughs at her boyfriend's expense.

"Joe," Heaven said looking around, "did you invite your body building friend, Kathy?"

"Yes, and I could tell she was touched that you included her. But she was going pheasant hunting in Nebraska."

"There's no accounting for what people do in their spare time," Heaven said. "My first husband loved to pheasant hunt. Quail, too."

"Mom, I'm going to hit a few gay bars with the guys," Iris said.

"But first, I think we have to dance a little here to get ready for the madness at the Dixie Bell," Joe Long said. "Can we put on Aretha?"

"We can. And James Brown. And then some Barry White to get you really prepared for the disco," Heaven said as she went over to the Bose CD player. "Let's dance," she yelled.

And they did. Mona and Sal even hit the dance floor for "Chain of Fools."

Finally Hank and Heaven were alone. The crowd had cleared out between eleven and midnight and two of Hank's friends from the neighborhood, a nice married couple Hank's age, had stayed and helped bus everything into piles. Hank and his friend had emptied the trash outside in the Dumpster so the house wouldn't smell like stale beer and wine in the morning. Then Heaven and Hank had loaded the dishwasher and turned it on, Heaven had poured herself one more glass of Veuve Clicquot, and they were now cuddling on the couch.

"How many people do you think were here during the evening?" Hank asked as he pulled off Heaven's cowboy boots.

"Seventy-five or eighty, I bet. We have great friends.

And I'm glad some of Iris's high-school friends showed up. They seemed to have a nice time."

"Even if Iris is part of European rock society, she's still a down-to-earth Midwestern American at heart. She and her friends seemed to pick up right where they left off. You did a good job with your daughter, Heaven."

"Stop saying nice things. I've already cried about ten times today, I've been so happy and sappy."

Hank went over to the tree and found a small package. He brought it back over to the couch and sat down, handing it to her. "I was going to put this in your stocking but I think you should open it now."

"You know I don't approve of opening presents on Christmas Eve," Heaven said, shaking the package.

"When you see this, you'll understand. And for your information, it's one in the morning. Christmas morning. Open it."

Heaven tore the package open and found two paintbrushes tied on two jars. The labels on the jars read, "Dark Chocolate Body Paint" and "Milk Chocolate Body Paint." She knew she was blushing. The room was dark but for the lights on the tree. She took Hank's hand and kissed it. "Come to think of it, I didn't have dessert tonight. Maybe we should put Barry White on and go upstairs. Iris won't be home for an hour or so."

"Merry Christmas, Heaven," Hank said as he picked up the jars of body paint and led her toward the stairs.

"I'm sorry Hank couldn't come with us," Iris said.

They were driving west on I-70, headed toward Heaven's childhood home in Kansas.

"Hank is used to not having weekends and holidays free and with all the hours I work at the restaurant, it isn't much of a problem for us. I'm just glad he got Christmas Eve off, and that he was able to spend the morning with his mother."

"How's that going?" Iris asked.

"She still hates me. She's a mother who managed to get her two children out of Vietnam just in time. Her husband was killed. She wanted something, wants something for Hank that doesn't include a girlfriend twenty years older than him."

Iris kept silent. It was snowing, not a lot, but big wet flakes were fluttering down, melting on the road when they hit.

Heaven looked over at her daughter. "I know what you're thinking and there's no doubt there's a karmic lesson in this for me. I don't like you being with Stuart, Mrs. Wing doesn't like me being with Hank. But I've been good this week, about Stuart I mean."

"Yes, you have. You've been polite and hospitable. Only someone who knew you would see how difficult it's been. Unfortunately, Stuart knows you. He knows you're acting."

"It's better than me throwing a fit, not letting him sleep with you, being boring and having a big talk with him and several other things I wanted to do," Heaven said defensively.

"Musicians are strange, aren't they?" Iris said, serious now.

"Well, as someone who has not only been married to one, but also was involved in managing and representing them, I certainly agree," Heaven said. "Musicians are strange. One of the things I find so interesting about them is that their creative activity is done with other creative people."

"Why does that interest you so much?"

156

"Think about it. A writer writes a book alone. A painter paints alone. Even a film director, it's his vision and only his vision that all the other crew members and actors are trying to get down on film. But a band is made up of five or six people who are all being creative at the same time. It's amazing that any song makes sense."

"No wonder bands are always fighting and breaking up, when you think about it that way," Iris said. "Something else that you taught me about musicians is that their art disappears every time they play. Of course, sometimes they're being recorded, but when they play a song that isn't being recorded and the notes hover in the air and then disappear, that version of the song is gone forever."

Heaven turned off the highway on an exit so familiar to her she did it automatically. "When you think about musicians like this, it's no wonder we both fell in love with one. It's so romantic, what with the creative collaboration and the songs lost in the universe's atmosphere forever. But listen, can we talk about the Foster situation before we get to Del's?"

"Why before we get there? Aren't you going to tell Uncle Del what's been going on?"

"Yes, but the short version. I don't want to bore everyone with all the gory details. What do you really think?"

"Well, it's hard to imagine two different murders that don't have anything to do with each other just happened to occur in the same week at the same company. Then there's the bugs and stuff. And I think Stephanie's Uncle David is a little creepy. I know he doesn't live in Kansas City and wasn't around for most of the trouble but he definitely has a grudge against his brothers. Maybe he paid someone to shoot down the blimp."

"And also kill Oliver Bodden and frame his brother for the murder? That sure would be good revenge, all right. And I do agree that he's still pissed, but that would take a ton of planning and what's in it for him, beside revenge? If he was going to inherit the company or millions of dollars, then I'd be all over him."

"Didn't you tell me once that most people are murdered by a loved one?"

Heaven turned into the driveway of her family farm. The dusting of snow was picture perfect over the barns and tractors. The house was outlined in colored lights and they were turned on, even though it was eleven in the morning. It was so corny Heaven thought she was going to cry right then. She couldn't, not after all the times she'd teared up the day before. Iris would think she was losing it. She exhaled air instead. "Yes, that used to be true. I'm not sure it is anymore, now that terrorist tactics have become so popular. Everyone likes to destroy buildings full of strangers to make their point nowadays. We're here," she said and honked the horn a couple of times.

"You always honked like that when I was a kid and we pulled in this drive. I love it out here," Iris said, then wagged her finger at her mother as they started to unload the van. "Don't you start crying yet."

Heaven pulled out a crate of champagne. "I'll try to wait until we get in the house at least. A white Christmas, honey. Aren't we lucky?"

Stephanie checked her watch again. How much longer did she have to stay? She was so exhausted from the last two weeks and she knew that the store would be busy again tomorrow. People were still giving each other chocolates for the holidays and now they'd be buying them for New Year's Eve parties. She watched her mom, dad, Aunt Carol and Uncle David playing gin rummy. Her other uncle, Carol's husband, was sleeping in her dad's recliner.

It had been a tough Christmas for Stephanie, her first since the divorce had been final. She'd been estranged last year, but she and her husband had seen each other on Christmas Day. Now it was real. She had almost asked Heaven if she could stay all night down on 5th Street, that's how much she didn't want to face Christmas morning alone. Instead she'd gone home and downed several belts of brandy, on top of the margarita and glasses of wine she'd consumed at the party. Getting out of bed had been difficult. Luckily she didn't have to cook anything. She'd just shown up with gifts and chocolate desserts. Now it was evening and she wanted so badly to go home and get in bed, she didn't even care if she'd be alone and pitiful.

The whole day had been tinged with melancholy anyway. Stephanie thought that her mother and aunt and uncle were more acutely aware of the rift in the family this year, having recently been assembled together with the brothers. Stephanie's grandmother had done her usual, she came to Stephanie's mom's first, then took off the minute lunch was over to go to Junior's. Junior and his and Claude's families ate their Christmas dinner in the evening. Stephanie's father took his mother-in-law and dropped her off at the front door of Junior's house. It was sad.

Suddenly Janie came around the corner, rage on her pinched face, slamming something down on the card table. It scared Stephanie because she was half asleep.

"Why," Janie said loudly, "do we have to have chocolate cake on Christmas? Why not pumpkin pie or mincemeat like other people?" She tipped the plate with the slice of cake over and smashed it into the table, catching a few cards in the frosting. "I hate chocolate!" she said and stormed out of the room.

For a while no one else moved or made a sound.

Heaven and Iris were on horseback, riding behind Del and his family, who were also on horseback. There was about two inches of new snow on the ground. It was something out of a picture postcard for Colorado or some other Western state, only this time it was Kansas that looked so lovely. They were riding on the Flint Hills side of the family farm.

One side of the property, the northern side, was farmland. The southern side was the start of the Flint Hills, cattle country. Del and his father before him raised crops on one side and cattle on the other. The family had gone south into the grazing land for a holiday ride.

"I got married for the first time right over there," Heaven said as she pointed to a hill just to their west. "There were horse and buggies and lots of folks came on horseback to the ceremony, and see that little chapel out on the hillock? The Presbyterian minister brought his fancy robes and married us right out there. It was quite a party."

Iris looked at her mother. "I always think of you as a rock-and-roll, urban girl. What a prairie bride you must have been."

"It's the most beautiful place, isn't it?" Heaven was lost in her memories of that day.

"You know how people used to say that the television show *Seinfeld* was about nothing? Well, this place is the *Seinfeld* of America," Iris said, without rancor.

"It might be about nothingness, but it's not about nothing," Heaven said as she looked out on the rolling plains covered with snow.

The horizon met the ground effortlessly, the color of both blending into the other. The bright blue sky of earlier in the day had dulled into a gray that popped out only slightly from the snowy plains. They had all cantered over a pasture, Iris and Heaven both squealing with delight and a little fear. Heaven only rode three or four times a year so she wasn't used to the power of a big horse running. Now they were almost back to the farm and the horses suddenly turned from an east/west direction to the north, where their barn was located.

The whole family rode into the barn and took the tack off the horses, fed them some Christmas oats and headed into the house. When they got inside, Heaven's purse was ringing.

Heaven didn't talk all the time on her cell phone, she thought it was tacky, but she felt much safer traveling around alone and driving home late at night from the restaurant with a cell phone in her bag.

"Hello and Merry Christmas," Heaven said. She paused and then said, "Thanks, Hank. We'll see you in a couple of hours. Me too." She clicked the phone off and looked at Iris. "We better go, honey."

"What's the matter, Mom?"

"Hank says Stephanie called him at the hospital. She said to call her as soon as we got back. Her cousin Jane stormed out of Christmas dinner. But that's not why he called." She didn't continue, though, staring out the window at the rolling hills, wanting to go back a couple of hours and stay there. She heard laughter coming from the kitchen, her sister-in-law Debbie rattling pans.

"What, Mom?"

"Someone broke every window at Café Heaven and wrote graffiti all over the front of the building."

"Did Hank see it?"

"No, Bonnie Weber called him. The patrol unit called her, knowing she was my friend. They didn't think anything inside had been touched. I guess someone wrote, 'Death Is Semisweet' all over the outside of Café Heaven."

Chocolate Marshmallow Gingerbread

1 pint dark molasses
9 oz. unsalted butter
½ cup strong coffee
½ tsp. salt
1 tsp. allspice
4 tsp. cinnamon
2 tsp. ground mace
1 tsp. clove
4 tsp. ground ginger
2 tsp. nutmeg
1 ½ tsp. baking soda
4 ¾ cups cake flour
3–4 cooking apples
3 T. brown sugar
1 pint sour cream
2 eggs
½ cup semisweet chocolate bits
1 cup miniature marshmallows
2 tsp. vanilla

Preheat oven to 350 degrees.

Combine 2 cups molasses, butter and ¼ cup coffee and heat to boil. As soon as it bubbles, remove from heat and let cool.

Combine dry ingredients except for brown sugar, chocolate bits and marshmallows.

Butter a 9-×-13-inch pan; peel apples and slice about ¼ inch thick. Cover the bottom of the pan with overlapping apple slices. Sprinkle with the brown sugar.

Blend the sour cream into the cooled molasses mixture. Combine with dry ingredients. Beat in eggs. Blend in chocolate, marshmallow and vanilla. Add the rest of the coffee to get a thick but pourable batter. Bake about 40 minutes, until a toothpick comes out dry in the center. Cool and serve in inverted squares so the apples are on top.

Eleven

The windows of Sal's barber shop were crowded with faces peering out. Mona, Joe, Murray, Heaven and Iris were there, and Sal, of course. Everyone was lined up watching the glass crew across the street replacing the windows in Café Heaven as if it were a play on a stage, put on for their amusement. Only no one was amused. The words, "Death is Semisweet" had been written in dark brown paint, paint the color of dark chocolate. They looked ominous.

"What did you do last night, Heaven," Sal asked, "camp out over there so no one would come in and help themselves to the vodka?"

Heaven, staring vacantly across the street, shook her head and took another piece of chocolate chip ginger-bread that Mona had brought in. They were all anxiety eating. "Hank had already called the glass service. Bonnie told him who to call. They work twenty-four hours, the glass people, because lots of barroom brawls and breaking and entering occur at night. By the time Iris and I got back from the farm—"

Murray broke in. "Hank called me and I came right down and met the glass guys, opened up. They nailed up these four-by-eight pieces of plywood for the night."

"—they were already almost done covering up the windows," Heaven continued.

"Securing the premises, they call it," Iris offered.

Mona sniffed. "I'm sorry. I just don't get it. What in the world do you have to do with all of this chocolate mess?"

"She's a friend of the Chocolate Queen," Murray offered.

"Who just happens to be related to the Fosters," Sal added. "And we know what's happened to the Fosters lately."

"Mom also let the police have a meeting of all the Foster family at the café," Iris said.

Joe, who'd been quiet until he'd finished two cups of coffee, was now ready to speculate. "And Heaven is one of the featured chefs at Foster's big chocolate party on New Year's Eve." He looked sharply at Heaven. "Don't tell me you're going to show up at that event after this."

Iris was nodding vehemently, obviously agreeing with Joe. "I told Mom last night they should cancel it. It would be just asking for trouble to have some big party sponsored by Foster's right now. Yes, Mom could get hurt, but there's also the possibility that everyone that attended could get mowed down with an automatic weapon or something. I'm beginning to think that the brother who got arrested for killing that African guy was framed. So many things have happened since then that I have this mental picture of a deranged chocolate hater out there, armed and dangerous."

Heaven left the window and flopped down on one of the many Naugahyde and chrome chairs that lined the barber shop. "Remember that brother Claude is out on bail. He could still be on some terror spree. But the deranged part I think is true, whoever it is. That's why I'm going to the hospital this morning. Hank had an idea last night." She stopped talking, deep in thought, and the whole room waited quietly for her to tell them Hank's idea.

After what seemed like hours but was just a few seconds, Sal cleared his throat loudly. "Are you gonna tell us or what?" he said gruffly.

Heaven started. "Oh, sorry. Well, Hank and Iris and I were discussing the fact that it seemed like someone really had a grudge against either chocolate in general or Foster's in particular and Hank suggested that Bonnie and I talk to a therapist who deals with eating disorders to see what a professional thought of the whole idea. Could a person be so fixated on a certain food that they'd actually kill because of it?"

"Right. I bet what Hank really said was that maybe Bonnie should consult an eating disorder shrink and somehow you stuck your nose in," Sal said as he laid out his combs and clippers.

Heaven folded her arms over her chest. "So? It's my restaurant that just got vandalized. I guess that puts me right in the middle of this. Besides, I sell food for a living. I'm curious about food crackpots, so this will benefit me as much as Bonnie."

"How did you get Bonnie to agree to you going along?" Mona asked, always in awe of her friend's chutzpah.

Heaven got up and stretched her arms. "Ouch. I'm sore from riding a horse yesterday. I asked Hank if he

167

could recommend someone over at the medical center. Then I asked him if he would call that person up early this morning and tell them that the police needed to consult with her, turns out it's a her, right away about a case. After he did that I called Bonnie and told her it was all set up, that we were going to see a food shrink about eating disorders at ten this morning."

"Smooth," Mona said, shaking her head.

"Iris, what did you get for Christmas from your mommy?" Joe asked, changing the subject.

Iris beamed. "My mommy is taking me to Paris in April, just the two of us."

"If the deranged chocolate killer doesn't get me first," Heaven said lightly. "Murray, I called the insurance man and he says my insurance covers the windows. Will you make sure the glass guys leave an invoice so we can give it to the insurance company?"

Murray held up his hands like he was on top of it. "I'm going to stand right here until they're done, and also make sure the painters get here and fix the graffiti. They said they wouldn't be here until mid-morning."

"Thank you and you can even charge me for your time. Iris, what are you going to do, honey?"

"I think Joe and I are going to go have a real breakfast at the Corner."

"Then I'm outta here. I'll come back to the restaurant as soon as we're done. Our meeting is at the hospital so I won't be too long," Heaven said and walked out the door.

"They've got to cancel that party," Iris said as she watched her mother cross the street.

. . .

"There's lots to choose from," Dr. Helen Walker said, tossing a paper across her desk toward Bonnie Weber and Heaven.

Bonnie took the page and looked up with a quizzical expression. "What's this?"

"A little article I found on the effects of chocolate on the human brain. At least three hundred known chemicals have been identified in chocolate. Most of these chemicals create good feelings."

Bonnie folded up the copy. "Can I take this with me to read later?"

"Yes, of course."

Heaven broke in, impatient. "Can you just give us the drift?"

"Well, the best known is probably caffeine, which is only present in chocolate in small quantities. But there's also another weak stimulant, theobromine. Then there's phenylethylamine, which is related to amphetamines. All of these increase the activity of neurotransmitters in portions of the brain that control our ability to pay attention and stay alert."

"Sounds like coffee. Is that all?"

Dr. Walker shook her head. "They've done some work out in San Diego. Chocolate may have something similar to THC, the active ingredient in marijuana, and that component could be creating the drug-induced psychosis that's associated with chocolate craving."

Bonnie beamed. "Now we're talking."

The doctor held up her hand. "It isn't exactly THC, it's called anadamide. The brain also produces anadamides naturally. All these neurotransmitters, such as anadamide and theobromine, break down quickly after they're produced by the brain. But there's some evidence that some other chemicals in chocolate inhibit the breakdown, so you feel better, longer. It's really amazing stuff."

"So is it addictive?" Heaven asked.

"Not physically, but certainly I've had some patients that were psychologically addicted."

"Do you have any right now?" Bonnie asked, knowing the doctor wouldn't want to share that information.

Dr. Walker smiled and shook her head. "Good try."

"Come on, doc, I've got two homicides and a string of vandalisms that are all focused on chocolate, and Foster's in particular," Bonnie said.

"I understand, and I will say that I don't have anyone I'm treating right now that comes right to mind."

"But if most of the things that chocolate does to our brains are things that we consider positive, why would anyone hate chocolate candymakers?" Heaven asked.

"Most of the people I treat, most people with eating disorders, have terrible self-esteem and self-worth issues. If you think of yourself as a bad person and chocolate makes you feel good, happy for a few minutes, then you have conflict about chocolate," Dr. Walker said.

"Sounds perfectly logical," Bonnie said as she stood up and put the article in her big purse. "I can see another Twinkie defense coming my way. Thanks for the information. If someone comes in and confesses to being the Foster's Chocolates killer, I don't suppose I'll be getting a call?"

"I will do my best to convince that individual to do the right thing," the doctor said enigmatically.

Heaven wiped her hands on the kitchen towel draped through her apron strings and picked up the phone. "Yes?"

"This is Marie Whitmer, from the executive offices at Foster's." The voice on the other end of the line sounded tense, worried.

"And this is Heaven Lee, but I guess you know that since you asked for me. We met the day that Claude was arrested. What's up, Marie?"

There was a pause. "The brothers wanted me to call you and let you know they have decided to cancel the event scheduled for New Year's Eve. They are afraid that either people wouldn't attend or if they did attend . . ." Silence.

"That something bad might happen to them?" Heaven offered.

"Exactly. The Fosters wanted all you chefs to know they will still donate the proceeds of the recipe book sales to the food bank and they hope to have a party at some time in the future, when all this quiets down."

"I think that's a good judgment call under the circumstances. No sense in getting other innocent people involved, eh, Marie," Heaven said, anxious to get back to the walnuts she was frying in olive oil. She made a gesture for Paula Kramer, the pastry chef and baker, to check them.

"Innocent people. Oh, God," the voice on the other end of the line said, cracking into sobs. "It's my fault."

"Marie, what are you talking about? I know it must be hard for you," Heaven said in her most soothing voice.

"I'll never forgive myself if poor Claude goes to jail," she said and then the phone went dead.

"Marie!" Heaven yelled. Was Marie just on edge because her job and her boss were both in jeopardy, or was she trying to confess? The kitchen phone rang again. Heaven considered just letting it ring. It was getting late and she needed to help with the prep. The café wasn't open for lunch this week between Christmas and New Year's Eve but they had lots of reservations for dinner.

She'd never been able to resist a ringing phone.

"What?" she said sternly as she answered, trying to indicate she was a busy woman.

"I'm at your back door. I have to go to the paper store, where we get our tissue and wrappers and stuff. Can you come with me?" It was Stephanie.

"Ha. I wish. I'm coming out," she said as she hung up the phone and walked out the kitchen door. Heaven slipped into the passenger's seat of Stephanie's old BMW which was already parked where the delivery trucks usually pulled up the alley. "I can't go anywhere. I'm behind. Did you see the outside of the restaurant earlier, before the painters?"

"Oh, yes. I was compelled by prurient interest to drive by on my way to work. I feel like I've brought you bad luck. Our whole family is falling apart and somehow you've been sucked into the vortex."

Heaven patted her friend's hand. "I didn't really get to talk to you last night, just that call from the car when Iris and I were rushing to get back to Kansas City. Tell me more about your cousin."

Stephanie rolled her eyes and smiled a half-hearted smile. "After lunch Janie disappeared for a while. I say that now, but I was so worn out I didn't notice yesterday. Her father and I were taking naps in our chairs and everyone else was playing gin rummy. I think she'd been in the kitchen secretly binging on chocolate cake and all of a sudden she came out, upended a piece of cake in the middle of the card table and raved about how she hated chocolate."

"At your mom's?"

"Yes, it was quite the scene. Everyone was telling her to sit down, telling her she must be overly tired, to have some tea. She dodged the whole pack and ran out the back door. The last I saw her she was running down the sidewalk without a coat, jumping into her car and whizzing away."

"Wow. She's had a meltdown. How is she today?" Heaven's mind was racing. Janie had just turned into a prime suspect.

"She's gone."

"What do you mean gone?"

Stephanie shrugged. "I mean no one has seen her or spoken to her since she left my mother's. Her folks are frantic. They had a key and went to her house but it didn't look like she'd been home. They've called the police—"

"But she hasn't been gone long enough for a missing persons report," Heaven finished Stephanie's thought. "I think we should let Bonnie know about this. When she tells the missing persons unit that Janie is involved in two homicides, they'll start looking for her."

"But she isn't exactly involved," Stephanie said defensively.

Heaven was practically jumping up and down in her seat. "Well, she's a member of the family and she obviously has problems about eating and chocolate and has a love-hate relationship with the product and her employers that must make her job difficult. Steph, maybe she's the one who's responsible for all this."

"You mean the blimp and Oliver Bodden and the bugs in the candy and all that?"

"And maybe after she left your family she came over to the café and broke the windows and wrote that stuff.

Before I knew she was your cousin I saw her eating a Foster's candy bar at that body building show I went to at Woodside. She was very guilty looking. Put that together with her former eating disorders and all the family feuding over the company. She could have fixated on destroying Foster's."

Stephanie looked sad. She glanced at her watch. "I have to get to this supply house before they close. Will you please call Bonnie?"

"Of course." She considered telling Stephanie about her conversation with the brothers' secretary but decided it could wait. Stephanie was overwhelmed right now with all this family stuff and running her own business. "What are you thinking?"

Stephanie put the car in reverse, her foot still on the brake. "I hope Janie is all right. If she's the one who did all this, and I hope you're wrong about it, but it does make sense, then she could have hurt herself, maybe commited suicide in a fit of Christmas guilt."

Heaven got out of the car and leaned her head back in to try to reassure her friend. "Maybe she just went to a cheap motel to gorge on her candy bars. She'll probably call soon," she said with a cheery wave as her friend backed down the alley.

She was never going to get her prep work done. The kitchen would be cross with her.

"Heaven, isn't it time for you to go back to the kitchen," Murray said, glancing at his watch for effect.

"It's only six," Heaven said as she stared at the door of the restaurant. "Did I describe her? Sixties, under five foot five, dark hair . . ."

"I know, supremely competent." Murray was able to

finish the list. "Don't you think this Marie Whitmer will ask to see you if she shows, which I'm not convinced she will?"

"Yes, I guess. I didn't even actually talk to her. I just left a message on her machine at work, asked her to come in, said it was very important. Stephanie hasn't called, has she?"

"Not since she called at five," Murray answered, trying to sound patient. "I'm sorry about her cousin."

"And her uncles and her whole family. I'm sorry for them all especially now that it looks like Janie was behind all this and framed her own uncle for one of the murders. Or maybe it's the secretary or dear Uncle David."

"What does Bonnie say about all this?" Murray asked.

"She said to butt out, that I'd already made somone mad enough to vandalize the café. Sometimes she's such a cop. She did lean on the missing persons unit to go by Janie's house and knock on the door, peer in the windows and ask a few questions of the neighbors, not that it did any good. People aren't real alert about comings and goings around the neighborhood on Christmas Day."

"I thought you asked Bonnie to be here, so she could swoop in on the secretary if she showed."

Heaven shrugged. "She had a homicide department Christmas party tonight and she chose that instead. Can you imagine? I'm sure she knows we can handle this."

Murray couldn't help laughing. "Oh, yeah. I'm sure that's just what Bonnie said."

"Heaven?" a voice called. She turned and saw Kathy Hager standing there. "I just wanted to stop by and thank you for inviting me to your Christmas party. It meant a great deal to me, and I'm sorry I was out of

town. The holidays have been tough for me since Courtney died, so your gesture was really sweet."

"Of course. I'm sorry you were out of town too. I understand how tough the holidays can be after losing
someone." At that Kathy's face crumbled. Her lip quiv-
ered. She sank onto a barstool near Heaven as if she was
unable to hold herself up anymore.

Heaven looked around. Murray had moved away from
them and was seating a four top. "Kathy, are you all
right? Can I get you a glass of water?"

"I'll be fine. Sometimes it just hits me again, her
death, being alone. And it all happened so unnecessarily." Her voice had turned angry.

Unnecessarily? Heaven didn't get that. "What do you
mean, unnecessarily? Breast cancer is tragic, but what
could anyone have done?"

"Well, it's complicated, but it didn't have to happen.
I know it could've been avoided. You see, the company
Courtney worked for was bought out by another company. The next day, the very next day, mind you, the
company closed the facility she worked at and laid off
everyone."

Heaven shook her head. She'd asked, now she had to
listen, although she still didn't see how a layoff caused
a death. "Companies can be so cold. That's why I've
tried to never work for big companies. How did this happen?"

"You know how a company is supposed to give you a
chance to keep your health insurance? Well, Courtney's
extension fell between the cracks. The policy was
dropped and she didn't know it until they found a lump
in her breast. When she went to work here in Kansas
City, that breast wasn't covered in her new insurance
because . . ."

"It was a preexisting condition," Heaven said. What a sad story. She looked around the room. Had Marie, the secretary, snuck in when she wasn't looking? "I guess without insurance you don't get a lot of options in your treatment."

Kathy smiled bitterly. "And because we were in a same-sex relationship I couldn't have her on my insurance at the university. She was screwed every way you look at it."

Heaven had to get to the kitchen. The room was filling up. She changed the subject. "Joe told me you went pheasant hunting. How'd you do?"

"Yeah, up in Nebraska with my son-in-law. I enjoy the heck out of it. We bagged ten pheasants and about thirty quail. It was relaxing to me."

Heaven thought about her father and brother going hunting at Thanksgiving and Christmas. It tugged at her. Familiar activities make you miss the people that used to do them, especially around the holidays. "Relaxing sounds good. I hope I get to do it again before I'm too old to enjoy myself."

Kathy jerked her head toward 39th Street. "I just happened to drive by here early this morning on my way back in town and all your windows were boarded up and the place was a mess. You sure did get it back together fast."

Heaven motioned to the bartender to come over. "It was just surface stuff that could be fixed. Talking about your partner really puts windows and graffiti in perspective. Kathy, I've got to get back to the kitchen. Let me buy you a drink. Tony, get Kathy whatever she wants," she said and made a quick exit, looking at the door one last time, hoping Marie Whitmer would show up soon.

• • •

Janie opened her eyes. She must have fallen asleep again and now she was stiff, cold. She wore a cotton blouse and jeans and the place that she'd been taken didn't seem to be heated. She tried to move her hands, which were tied behind her back. The skin on her fingers was cracked, her knees were skinned, her lips were pulled tight and parched by the duct tape. She hadn't had any water in days, or was it just a few hours? She rolled over on her face and tried to get up on her knees. Her ankles were also tied together but she had wiggled a little play in the rope. She curved her toes to push against the floor slightly and rose up to her knees, trying to get a better sense of where she was. It was dark but nothing could wipe out the smell. There was paper all over the floor. It crackled as she moved. Even before her captor had turned on the light she knew what was around her. When had that been? The light? The feeding?

The thought of that, the forced feeding, turned Janie's stomach. She gagged and sank back down on the floor, rolling over on her back and her raw, skinned hands, gasping for air. She could hear someone walking above her. Had that walking been going on all the time, or was it a new sound?

She felt hope and dread in about equal proportions. Where was she and how could she escape?

Chocolate Martini

2 parts vodka
1 part Godiva chocolate liqueur
1 splash cold espresso coffee
1 chocolate-covered coffee bean

Mix all the ingredients together over ice, shake and strain into martini glasses. Garnish with a chocolate-covered coffee bean.

Twelve

I'm a failure," Heaven stated dramatically. She took another bite of a chocolate-covered cherry she'd found in a box of chocolates on Sal's counter. Sal's regular customers gave him holiday gifts.

"You don't do that right," Sal proclaimed.

"What right?"

"Eat the chocolate-covered cherry. You have to put the whole thing in your mouth and then bite into it. Everybody knows that."

Heaven flourished her half-eaten cherry around, getting some of the filling on her hand in the process. "I like to live dangerously, Sal, everybody knows that," she said, putting the rest of the candy in her mouth, licking the sticky spot on her hand quickly, hoping Sal wouldn't catch her.

"Stop that and wash your hands in the next sink," Sal ordered without looking around.

Sal had two hair-cutting stations in his shop complete with barber chairs and running water and those sinks with indentations for the neck. Sometimes he went back and forth between two customers. Right now he just had the bartender from the biker bar down 39th Street in his main chair, trimming his beard.

Heaven did as she was told and washed her hands.

"Now, what's this I'm-a-failure bull," Sal said gruffly.

"I haven't helped. Janie, who I'm sure is the culprit, has disappeared. But there is no actual proof that she did anything more than go a little off at Christmas dinner. So maybe it *isn't* her and maybe it's Uncle David, who I'm sure has been harboring a grudge all these years. And then yesterday the secretary at Foster's called to tell me there wasn't going to be a New Year's Eve party and she started talking about how she'd never forgive herself if Claude was found guilty. I was pretty sure if I could get her to the restaurant she'd confess to something, but she didn't show up. No one has come forward to say they saw her, Janie, David, or anyone else for that matter, breaking the windows across the street at my café or painting stuff on the building. And this is a busy street. Claude is still indicted for manslaughter but I'm pretty sure he didn't do it. I can't make any of the pieces fit together."

"I'm just glad they canceled the damn chocolate party. That would've been asking for it."

"Me too. Did I tell you we're going to be open tomorrow?"

"Murray told me. How'd that happen?"

"Since New Year's Eve is on a Sunday I let the staff decide. Did they want to open and make money or stay closed and spend money? They decided they wanted to work and that's all right with me. We'll need the bucks for sales tax in January."

"Where's Iris?"

"Picking up her boyfriend at the airport. They're going off to Bali next week," Heaven said, letting Sal know by her tone of voice she wasn't happy about it.

"Let it go, H." Sal brushed loose hairs off the neck of the bartender. "She's a good kid. It could be a lot worse. He could be an old druggie musician and not be rich as a lord. I guess he's both, rich and a lord."

Heaven was staring out the window, not really listening to Sal, although she knew what he was saying. Suddenly she jumped up, pointing her finger toward the west. "That's her. That's Marie Whitmer," she shouted and ran out the door.

Marie was walking purposefully down 39th Street, her handbag held tightly in front of her with both hands. She was looking at the address numbers on the businesses, as if she had no idea where Café Heaven was.

Heaven ran across the street to intercept her. "Marie, where have you been?"

Marie was startled but she stopped and nodded to Heaven. "I have been battling with this. I told my husband not to answer the phone. There were several calls from that woman detective. What did you tell her?"

Heaven glanced over at Sal's. He was watching her through the window intently, as if this little sixty-year-old lady was going to jump on Heaven. She waved at Sal, then smiled at Marie. "Let's go in my restaurant and have a cup of coffee. We don't have to talk out here on the street," she said, and started to walk toward the café. Marie followed, still clutching her purse.

As soon as they entered the café, Heaven sat Marie down, ran in the kitchen and grabbed some chocolate cake, poured two cups of coffee, went back in the kitchen and grabbed some half-and-half and came back in the dining room.

"I couldn't eat that," Marie said, her eyes filling up with tears. "It's chocolate. It reminds me of the mess Claude is in because of me."

Heaven took the offending cake back in the kitchen without a word. "Quick, what else do we have sweet that's not chocolate?" she whispered to Pauline Kramer.

"Pumpkin cheesecake," Pauline said and reached in her pastry cooler. She expertly cut two slices and handed them to Heaven who took them and tried Marie again.

This time Marie sniffed and took a small bite with her fork, nodding her head in appreciation. "I know you think you can help me but we might as well just call up that Bonnie Weber person and have her take my statement."

Heaven was excited. So the secretary did it. "Marie, I think you should have a lawyer present. I'm sure Bonnie, Sergeant Weber, would tell you the same thing."

Marie looked at Heaven with a puzzled expression. "I can't imagine why. I was just trying to be helpful."

Heaven thought she'd heard wrong. "Well, it's hard to imagine how downing an airship and killing Oliver Bodden would be exactly helpful, but I'm sure you had your reasons. Did the brothers take you for granted?"

Marie Whitmer stood up, looking at Heaven strangely, and picked up her purse. "I think I need to talk to my son. He's an attorney. I will call you later today."

"No, Marie. Don't go," Heaven practically wailed. "You can tell me everything."

Marie was already opening the door to 39th Street. She never looked back.

It was too quiet.

Heaven had come home to change clothes and say hi

to Iris. As she fretted about Marie, she'd spilled an entire two-pound sour cream container full of raspberry dressing on her chef's coat, her tights and her shoes and socks. Even with the extra chef's coat she had at the restaurant, the rest of her outfit was sticky. She started up the stairs and peeled off the outer layer of clothing, calling out as she went. "Iris? Stuart?"

When she got to the top of the stairs, she knew she'd made a mistake. The door to Iris's room was open and she could see her daughter lying in bed, naked and asleep in a tangle of covers. She and Stuart must have come back to the house and made love. Heaven was embarrassed. She should have called before she came home in the middle of the day. She walked softly toward her own room when she heard a cough come from the bathroom.

When Heaven had redone the living quarters of the bakery, she'd put a rather glamourous bathroom in her suite, and redone the existing bathroom between the two rooms in the hall for Iris. Each woman had a studio or office space, a giant bedroom and their own bathroom. Iris's just happened to be down the hall a little bit from her bedroom.

Heaven stopped in front of the door to this bathroom. Something wasn't quite right. She supposed Stuart was in there and it was certainly none of her business but there it was, smoke coming out from under the door. She tried the door and it opened.

The scene surprised her. "You asshole," she hissed.

Stuart Watts was leaning against the shower, smoking a huge joint. He turned around and smiled at Heaven. "Hello, love. As I remember, you like to toke a bit. Want some?"

Heaven closed the door to the bathroom behind her

and slid down on the floor next to the wall. Her legs were shaking. She breathed in the sweet smell of expensive marijuana. "Please don't tell me you put my daughter in danger by flying across the ocean with this shit. Please don't tell me that."

"Of course not, love. I got it from my son when I was on the coast. Calm down," he said and took a big toke.

Heaven could almost feel the way it was relaxing his muscles, his brain sending signals of well-being to the rest of his body.

He turned and held out the joint to her. "Come on, love, I know you want to."

Heaven got to her feet and opened the bathroom door. "I've got to get back to work," she said tiredly.

She put on clean clothes and left the house as fast as possible. She wouldn't chance changing her mind.

"Heaven, that woman finally showed," Joe said at the pass-through window. "Marie something. Murray said to tell you." He grabbed three Blu Heaven salads from the window and disappeared.

Heaven looked around helplessly. It was eight-thirty on a Saturday night and she was on the saute station, along with the lunch chef who was working nights this week. "Brian, I swear to God I will only be gone five minutes or you can come out and pull me back by my hair."

"Go," Brian said and took one of her saute pans full of scallops and moved it nearer to him.

Heaven, usually happy to see what was going on in the dining room, tried not to look to the left or the right, tried not to make eye contact with customers or employees. Marie Whitmer was standing next to a nice-looking young man in his thirties, short brown hair, sport jacket, serious demeanor. This must be the lawyer son, Heaven thought. She didn't wait for introductions. "Marie, I'm glad you came back but this is a really bad time. I actually cook in my own restaurant so do you want to eat something at the bar and wait until I can talk or what? Did Bonnie talk to you? I told her about our conversation earlier." She turned to the son and held out her hand. "Hi, there. I'm Heaven Lee."

The son picked up on the urgency, shaking hands briefly. "Paul Whitmer, and I've made an appointment with Sergeant Weber, but my mother insisted on talking to you first. She has an elevated view of the importance of what she did vis à vis giving out information. I doubt very much that this has anything to do with the problems that have befallen Foster's."

What was this giving out information line? "I'm afraid I don't understand. I thought your mother had something to confess?" Heaven wished she'd written down exactly what Marie had said to her.

The son looked at his mother and continued. "Foster's bought a company in Philadelphia several years ago, Smithson's Samplers. It was quite famous but badly run. Foster's closed it and laid off most of the staff. An employee of that company died of cancer a few years after the buyout and a grief-stricken loved one of that employee befriended my mother over the phone and over the years, asked her questions about Foster's. The answers to those questions were probably not for public consumption. Their initial contact was because the employees' insurance had not been properly extended and due to that there were some problems with the health-care. The loved one didn't blame my mother for this, or Foster's, it seemed. It had been mishandled at the

Philadelphia end. My mother actually helped the loved one to receive compensation from the insurance company. Of course, the former employee was still dead, compensation couldn't change that. But my mother and the loved one continued their phone calls long after the problem was dealt with. Mother now feels some of the questions this person asked and she answered were not appropriate for someone outside the company."

Heaven took a big breath. She had a million questions and no time. Obviously she and Marie had been talking about different things. "I understand that you want to protect your mother legally. But I have no legal standing whatsoever so talking to me doesn't count. Could you tell me the name of the person your mother talked to?" Now Heaven turned toward Marie. "I don't suppose Janie Anderson or David Foster fit that description?" All of her suspects were going down in one fell swoop.

Marie looked at her like she was crazy. "No, it was a woman named Kathy Hager. It's a little embarrassing for me to talk about this because the person in her life, the person who died, was another woman. Kathy was so nice and she was just brokenhearted, I can tell you that. I didn't give it too much thought, but now, remembering things she said . . . I don't think for a minute Kathy would do anything destructive but she did know about Oliver Bodden and the blimp ahead of the time those things were public knowledge. As I said she was a very nice women, even if she was a—"

Paul Whitmer held up his hand. "Mom, I'm sure this Kathy Hager has nothing to do with the Foster mess. But we came here because you felt uneasy and we'll tell the police, just in case."

Heaven took Marie Whitmer's hand and kissed it, much to the older woman's surprise. "Tony, will you get my friends a chocolate martini on me," she said and then realized that was probably pushing the chocolate theme too far. "Or whatever they want, please," she yelled at the bartender over the din. "I'm sure your son is right. You didn't give away any state secrets and you can't be responsible for what Kathy or your bosses have done. I've got to go. Thank you," Heaven said as fast as she could. She found Murray talking to a six top and smiled at the guests while pulling him aside. "Call Bonnie and beg her to meet me here at ten-thirty, after she talks to Marie. I should be able to get out of the kitchen by then. And ask Joe if he knows where Kathy Hager lives."

"I don't know, H. You know the law. The house is pitch dark. If you can't observe a crime being committed, how can you justify breaking in to stop a crime? Are you sure this is the right address?"

Heaven held up a cocktail napkin with writing on it to show Bonnie. "Joe has one of those electronic address books, so yes, I'm sure this is the right place. Remember why we decided to make this a casual visit, just you and me instead of a formal police thing? So we could improvise. We turn on some lights if we need to later and say whatever it takes. Bonnie, Kathy may be in there and just asleep. When we knock on the door she'll probably let us in and we'll take a look around and find out she's a messy housekeeper or she keeps girlie porn but I'm sure we won't find Janie."

Bonnie opened her car door and got out. "Then why are we here?" she asked sourly. "This Kathy Hager never mentioned to you that she was hooked up in any way with Foster's and to me, that stinks. Even when she told you about her lover's insurance problems she didn't say that it was caused by the evil Foster's Chocolates and, boy, am I glad they've had a patch of bad luck." She looked over the top of her car at Heaven. "Why are you backpedaling? Are you scared?"

"Of course not. Did I mention she went pheasant hunting so she must know how to shoot a gun?"

"Yes, and I mentioned that you shoot pheasants with a shotgun, not a rifle like what took down the airship. But it does establish that she can shoot at least one type of gun and the fact that you brought it up right now establishes that you're scared."

Heaven slammed her car door and marched up the sidewalk toward the house, head held high, not looking back at Bonnie. "Nice house. Brookside is a nice neighborhood."

Bonnie hurried to catch up to her friend. "Slow down. Let me do the talking," she barked as she climbed the steps to the front porch. "Kathy, hello, Kathy Hager," she called, knocking on the front door.

Heaven peered in the front windows of the house. "I see a couch, two leather chairs."

Bonnie gestured to her. "Get away from that window. You know better than that."

"Try the door," whispered Heaven.

Bonnie's hand moved instantly down to the doorknob and when it turned, she held up her hand for Heaven to stop. "Stay here. It may be a set-up."

"She probably just forgot. Probably goes in and out the back door," Heaven said, doubting her own words. What if Bonnie was killed or wounded because of her? "Pull your gun," she hissed.

Bonnie waved her Smith & Wesson at Heaven, already by her side. "Stay here," she said and opened the door and stepped inside with her weapon in front of her. She turned on all the light switches by the front door, lighting up the front porch, the entry hall and the living room. "Kathy Hager. Are you all right?" Silence. The house felt empty. She stepped back to the door and smiled at Heaven. "You followed my orders for once. How refreshing."

"This was a bad idea," Heaven said as she stepped into the hall. "One of my really bad ideas. Maybe we should call for backup."

Bonnie was already in the living room and headed for the kitchen. "Stay with me now. Be close to the one with the gun." She turned on the lights in the dining room as they passed through. An arched doorway without a door led to the kitchen. She found the light right inside the arch and they peered in at a tidy, clean kitchen with President plates displayed around the top of the cabinets. "I haven't seen President plates since grade school," Bonnie observed.

"The whole house has a retro feel to it," Heaven remarked. "I haven't seen an Early American dining-room set for a while either. I'm surprised there weren't crocheted doilies on the chairs. Maybe I'm all wrong on this, Bonnie."

Bonnie Weber had already moved toward the bedroom wing of the house, gun still out. "Stick close," she said softly, opening the first door. "Bathroom," she said. Heaven caught up with her for the next door opening. It was a home office with a computer station, a file cabinet and a bookshelf filled with lots of photos of Kathy and a pretty, feminine-looking woman with long, curly, strawberry-blond hair. There were also photos of the strawberry blonde in a baseball hats and turbans. It was clear she had lost the beautiful locks, Heaven supposed during some form of chemotherapy. There were also a dozen trophies from body building contests on the bookshelf.

Bonnie went to the last door at the end of the hall and opened it, Heaven right behind her. It was clearly the master bedroom. The bed was made, the comforter fluffed, the television turned off, the shoes and dirty clothes put away somewhere. Bonnie turned on the light in the closet and master bath as well as the bedroom. "Her closet is still full. If she ran, she didn't take clothes with her from this closet."

Heaven opened a drawer in a wooden bureau. It was full of tee shirts. "Same here. Maybe Kathy went to the grocery store and just forgot to lock the front door."

"At eleven-thirty at night?"

Heaven shrugged. "That's why they have twenty-four-hour stores. Someone uses them. Did you see a door to the basement? Most of these Brookside houses have basements."

"Let's go back to the kitchen," Bonnie said and as they headed down the hall they spotted a door tucked in the entryway area that Heaven had taken for a coat closet during the first tour. Bonnie quickly opened it. "Well, well, what do we have here?" she said as she flipped on the light. There were stairs leading down.

Heaven bent down and peeked. She saw a washer and dryer. "I hate this part. This is always where the detective gets jumped by the homicidal maniac."

Bonnie held her gun out in front of her. "Put your hand loosely on my shoulder and let's go," she ordered and they quickly went down the stairs. There was another light switch on the wooden beam at the bottom of the staircase and Bonnie flipped that on. As well as the laundry area, the basement had a workshop with a pegboard wall hung with tools, coffee cans full of nails and a work table built from a four-by-eight piece of plywood. Back in the corner was a small door.

Heaven straightened up from the crouch she'd been in coming down the stairs, looking around with relief. "Just a normal basement. No torture chamber or chain saw or anything. Let's go."

"Are you thinking of that old case where the guy escaped from a house just wearing the dog collar and nothing else?" Bonnie asked. "And the killer cut up his victims in the basement? I worked that case. Let's just check this little door. Probably full of Christmas decorations."

Heaven shuddered. "Bonnie, did you notice? There wasn't one holiday decoration upstairs? The house was totally Midwest traditional. Why wasn't there a Christmas tree?"

"You told me she said she wasn't in the holiday spirit," Bonnie said as she walked carefully toward the small door. She tried it and it was locked.

Heaven had moved over behind Bonnie. "That's weird. Usually these canning rooms aren't locked up." Using the phrase canning room jolted Heaven's memory. "Bonnie, do you remember when that darling little old lady tried to kill me in her canning room?"

Bonnie nodded her head, then threw her weight into pushing at the door. From the other side, there was movement, the rustling of paper. "Hello, this is Detective Bonnie Weber. Is someone in there?

Muffled sounds. "That sounds like a person trying to talk," Heaven said. "Let me help you with this door." She threw herself against it but it didn't give. However, the weight of Heaven's body jarred the door frame enough that a key fell off the top of the doorjamb to the floor.

Bonnie scooped up the key and grinned. "Now I know why I let you come with me on these jobs." She leaned over, working the lock, and shortly the little door popped open toward the main room of the basement. Bonnie straightened up and looked at Heaven. "We're almost done," and she felt around inside the open door for a light switch. As she stepped in the darkness, the smell overwhelmed her. "H, come here."

"Oh, my God. It must be a chocolate cellar," Heaven said as she stood in the door, breathing in deeply. "Try the middle of the room. Usually there's a lightbulb hanging in the middle of the room."

"You're now an expert on canning rooms," Bonnie said with a chuckle. She stepped deeper into the room and her foot hit something soft. "Oh, shit. Stay there." In just a second, the lightbulb was turned on and Bonnie and Heaven saw Janie Anderson, trussed up like a Christmas turkey on the floor covered with candy wrappers, her face and body soiled with chocolate. As Bonnie reached down to pull the duct tape off Janie's mouth, Heaven looked around the small room, lined with every kind of chocolate she could think of. "Bonnie, this place is a stash. Look, there must be a hundred pounds of Scharffenberger over there."

"Water," Janie moaned, her eyes fluttering.

Bonnie looked up at her from where she was kneeling beside Janie. "H, do you have your cell?"

"In the car," Heaven said.

"Then get the hell up the stairs, find a phone and call 911. And be careful. You can ogle the chocolate later. Bring some water and a blanket."

Vegetarian Chili with Chocolate

1 15–oz. can kidney beans
1 15–oz. can garbanzo beans
2 15–oz. cans black beans
1 15–oz. can diced tomatoes with the liquid, or 2 cans Rotel
    tomatoes and jalapeños
1 onion, peeled and chopped
1 yellow pepper, chopped
2 stalks celery, diced
2–6 cloves garlic diced, according to taste
2 jalapeños, seeded and sliced
1 package chili seasoning
1 tsp. cinnamon
2 oz. bittersweet chocolate, broken up

This is a wonderful meatless dish first created by playwright Phil Blueowl Hooiser.

Drain the beans and throw everything but the chocolate into a slow cooker for 6–8 hours on low. Add a cup of water if it's too thick. Stir in the chocolate about an hour before serving.

Thirteen

I wish Sal was open," Heaven said as she looked over at the barbershop from the front windows of Café Heaven. She and Bonnie Weber were eating vegetarian chili with chocolate in it and Diet Cokes. It was ten in the morning on New Year's Eve.

"It's Sunday, Sal's only day off. What's the matter, don't you think we'll be able to think on this side of the street?" Bonnie teased.

"Thanks for coming over here," Heaven said, ignoring the jibe. "I had to stay put. I came in at eight and everyone else came in at nine. We have lots of prep to do for tonight."

"Are you having your usual floor show?"

"Oh, yes. Chris and Joe asked for a hundred bucks last week for costumes. I'm afraid to ask."

"So, I guess you want to know what Janie Anderson said when she got hydrated and calmed down."

"Every word."

"It will be disappointing to a drama queen like you.

No big confrontation. She drove home and even though it was barely five it was getting dark and as we know from Stephanie, Janie had acted out at the Christmas dinner so she was in an agitated state and probably wasn't watching her surroundings. Let that be a lesson to us all. She got out of the car and Kathy evidently had been watching her house, waiting. She came up behind Janie with chloroform or something like it on a rag. Kathy is strong; Janie was caught off guard. She just remembers being grabbed from behind and this smelly rag put over her face. When she woke up she was in the chocolate cellar. She still didn't know who had snatched her until the next day sometime when Kathy came down, smacked her around and crammed chocolate down her throat for a few minutes then left. She called Janie a Foster's bitch but didn't say much else. I'll talk to her again tomorrow when she gets out of the hospital. Her folks are going to take her to their house and they promise to get her in therapy. I told them about the food specialist at the Med. Center. Everything Janie told me was a little sketchy, unfortunately. Janie isn't the best witness on a good day, and this isn't a good day."

Heaven pulled out a cocktail napkin from her chef's jacket pocket. "I'm guessing you haven't found Kathy?"

"You guessed right. What've you got there?"

"A list. First crime: the airship incident. Kathy Hager is certainly muscular enough to look like a boy-type Santa in a Santa suit with some padding."

Bonnie nodded. "Yes and I suppose knowing she can shoot a shotgun could lead to the assumption that she could be good enough with a rifle for the airship hit. It's a stretch but I think we can put a small check on that one."

Heaven took a pen out of her pocket and made a big

check. "Now, the death of Oliver Bodden. Kathy was strong."

"She could have knocked him unconscious, pushed him in the chocolate, and then pulled the wire tight, yes."

Heaven made another check. "Stephanie has never met Kathy, to my knowledge. In all the bustle at the Chocolate Queen last week she could have slipped some larvae in the back room storage containers and she wouldn't have recognized her as anything but a random customer."

"What about the bad chocolate at Foster's?"

"I don't know how she could have pulled that one. Unless the secretary let Kathy come into the building?"

Bonnie slapped Heaven on the shoulder. "Marie Whitmer. That's probably why she's feeling so guilty. I'll have to talk to her son, the lawyer."

"So I'll put a check by the bugs and a question mark by the bloom at the factory."

"The graffiti and the windows here at the café have to get another question mark. We don't have anything to tie Kathy to that."

"Oh, please. Who else could it be? She knew I was friends with Stephanie and that I was going to be a chef for the Foster's party. It must be her."

"It most likely is but we don't have any proof. Actually we don't have one eyewitness for any of this," Bonnie pointed out. "You were hot for Janie as the perp just yesterday. And she is deluded. Maybe she broke into Kathy's house and set her up to conceal her own guilt."

"And duct taped her own mouth and tied herself up? Come on, Bonnie," Heaven said impatiently.

Bonnie got up. "I'm just bringing up a point. We don't have jack. I believe as you do that Kathy Hager has the best motive so far. And she's missing and her daughter in Omaha says she told her she was going on a retreat for Christmas. She didn't go pheasant hunting with the son-in-law."

Heaven stacked the dishes and loaded them on her arm. "Have they heard from her?"

"Neither daughter has heard from her since Christmas Day, when she told them she was in Atchison, Kansas, at a Benedictine monastery."

"Kathy Hager is the one. I just know it, but you're right, I just knew it was Jane Anderson until last night. I'm glad you're the detective, not me."

Bonnie headed for the door. "I'll remind you you said that. I hope I don't see you until next year," she said as she left.

Heaven had folded a white napkin around her head as a sweatband. The kitchen was swamped. It was eleven and the last round of guests had been seated. They were turning out mostly starters right now, salads, patés, snails and blini with caviar. Heaven had ordered some lobes of foie gras for the evening and on her station she seared the liver in a dry pan with some kosher salt. Then she put it on a thin slice of toast, topped it with some caramelized onions and some mango chutney that she'd made the day before. She was also doing a wild mushroom stroganoff at her station, sauteing a mixture of wild mushrooms and adding a little lemon juice and sour cream at the last minute, serving it on a thicker piece of toast with a little fresh dill on the top. She had ten pans of those two starters going at the same time. And she was smiling. "I love it when we're in the weeds but you can see the way out," she said.

Brian Hoffman, standing next to her, working the pasta station, looked over. "This is sure different from lunch," he said as he worked with five or six plates.

"What a wuss," Heaven said. The bravado of the line was like electricity running through her veins.

Joe Long stuck his head into the pass-through, picking up a couple of foie gras and some blini. "Heaven, I know you don't want to hear this, but Murray says Stuart Watts is on the phone and he says he must talk to you, that it's an emergency."

Heaven thought of the scene in the bathroom the other day and felt her stomach turn. She hoped Iris was all right, that drugs weren't involved. She didn't even argue, just went over to the phone in the kitchen. "What?" she bellowed over the din.

"Heaven, is Iris there with you?" Stuart asked, voice strained.

"I haven't seen her, why?"

"She left here about a half hour ago. There was a phone call saying you had been burned in a kitchen accident, that she was to go to the Medical Center."

"What? Who was the call from?"

"I have no idea. We were going to come down to the café for dinner and the show at midnight. We were almost ready. She said she'd call me and let me know what was happening. I haven't heard from her since."

"Stuart, I'm fine, plus I have a restaurant full of people who want to be fed so I need your help. Will you please call this number and tell Sergeant Bonnie Weber what you just told me? She was planning to stay home with her family tonight. If she doesn't answer, leave a detailed message, please. Then come down here to the café," Heaven said and gave him Bonnie's home phone number plus her cell phone number. "And call Hank and make sure Iris isn't sitting in the ER, waiting for me to show up," she added, giving him Hank's cell phone number. She knew Iris wasn't at the hospital because she'd have come down to the restaurant by now or at least called, to make sure her mother was all right.

"So the call was bogus?" Stuart asked.

"I haven't had an accident but I wouldn't say I'm fine after hearing this. I'm worried sick and I have to go." She hung up the phone and hurried back to her station, her heart heavy. She knew this was somehow connected to Kathy Hager and she kept seeing that room with all the chocolate in it at Kathy's house. Was her daughter there now, bound and gagged? Did Bonnie have a stakeout, police watching Kathy's house? She probably couldn't justify it. Woodenly, Heaven filled plates and saute pans and kept cooking. She didn't know what else to do.

The kitchen was set up so the line faced the dining room of the restaurant. At busy times like tonight, no one was paying attention to the back door of the kitchen because they were all facing the other direction.

So no one really knew what actually happened next.

A rock came crashing through one of the high, narrow windows. At the same time, a Molotov cocktail rolled across the kitchen floor and burst into flames; whether it was tossed in the unlocked door or came in the window after the rock, no one could say. As luck would have it, there was a small grease spill on the floor by the baking station near where the bottle fell and that patch burst into flames. The cooks were basically cut off from the kitchen door by a small conflagration.

They all turned around at the same time. "Shit," Heaven said and grabbed one of the fire extinguishers. She was able to put out the smaller fire right away. Jumpin' Jack, who was working salads, was beating at the larger fire with several rags, others were stomping on the fire, around the edges of the flames.

At that moment Heaven heard the sound of cries from the front of the house. "Keep working on it," she said to her coworkers as she rushed out into the dining room and saw two small fires on the floor by the front windows, broken glass shards catching the light and showing the path taken into the restaurant by the missiles. Tony the bartender was rushing over with a fire extinguisher. Luckily, neither of these gasoline-filled bottles landed on a table or the lap of a guest.

"Murray," Heaven yelled. He came running to the back. "The same thing happened in the back. Did you call 911?"

Murray shook his head. "Not yet. I think we'll get this out."

"Even if you do, call Bonnie. Do you think we should evacuate and shut down for the night?"

"Before the show?"

Heaven grabbed Murray's arm. "Iris is missing. I think Kathy Hager has grabbed her just like she did Stephanie's cousin. What's going to happen next?"

"You mean are the guests in danger from something else?"

"That's what I mean. And I don't know that I would want to stay in a place that had just been firebombed. Think about it. I'm checking the fire back in the kitchen."

"Heaven, telephone," Brian Hoffman said as she raced back in the kitchen. "They said it was an emergency. Pretty funny. What do we call what we've got here?"

The fire in the kitchen was almost out, the kitchen

being accustomed to having small fires. Most of the staff had retreated out into the alley to escape the black acrid smoke and the smell of gasoline. The floor was covered with baking soda, flour and other flame inhibitors. Jack was throwing kitchen towels on the floor around the fire area. Heaven grabbed the phone. "Stuart, did you hear from Iris?"

It wasn't Stuart. "Did you like the fireworks?" someone asked.

"What do you want?" Heaven said, suddenly so tired she thought she would buckle.

"It's what do you want. If you want your daughter, and your friend the little Miss Chocolate Queen, then meet me at the Foster's factory. No cops," the female voice said. Heaven was sure it was Kathy. Before she could say a thing, the line was dead.

Heaven turned to Jumpin' Jack. "I think we should call it a night. I'm going to tell Murray. You all try to clean up the place. I have to go."

"Go? You're *leaving*?"

"They were right, it's an emergency," she said, heading for the dining room. "Murray," she yelled.

The fires were out, the front door was open and several tables of guests were continuing their dining, perhaps thinking the pyrotechnics were just a part of the floor show gone awry. Murray looked quizzically at his boss.

"Kathy Hager has Iris and Stephanie at the Foster's plant. Did you get ahold of Bonnie?"

"Just her machine."

"Keep trying her cell and home. Call 911 and tell them to meet me there but they must be careful. She may have booby trapped the place. Come to think of it, don't call 911. She did say no cops, not that I intend on obeying. I'll call them when I get there."

"What should I do about the rest of the night?"

"Get the guests out of here. It's eleven-thirty. Who knows what she might have planned for midnight. Make an announcement. Tell people to give us their names and addresses and we'll send them a gift certificate for another dinner. This is going to cost a fortune," Heaven said. "But I can't worry about that now. I have to go."

Murray shook his head. "You can't go by yourself."

"I have to. I'll call you soon," Heaven said.

At that moment, a hook and ladder truck pulled up in front, lights flashing and sirens on full blast. Firefighters in yellow rubber gear poured in the door of the restaurant. Murray turned around to ask Heaven what to do but she was gone.

Heaven was surprised to find the gates of Foster's factory open. Surely after all the events of the past few weeks they'd hired security. She drove through and parked by the front door, jumped out of the van and found the front doors locked. She ran around the side of the building toward the new wing, looking for an opening. The big sliding doors were open. She could see Kathy Hager bending over a piece of equipment inside.

Heaven slipped quietly into the big room. It was dark except for a light over the equipment that Kathy was standing by. She knew she couldn't sneak up on her, that she would inevitably stumble on something. So she decided to declare herself. "Where's my daughter?" she yelled.

"Right over here, Heaven. I'm having to adjust this

machine manually to get the conveyer belt to repeat itself. But don't get any ideas that you can take me." Kathy Hager had a shotgun in her left hand, her right on the machine. She pointed the gun at Heaven waist-high like a Western sheriff. "Just because I didn't go pheasant hunting last week doesn't mean I don't know how to shoot this thing, and a rifle too. But you know that. Come a little closer so you can see what I'm working on."

Heaven took a few steps toward the other woman. On the conveyer belt in front of Kathy, Heaven saw Iris and Stephanie, tied down to the belt like it was a railroad track with duct tape on their mouths. They were both still fully clothed but an outer layer had been added. They were three-quarters covered with chocolate, starting with their shoes and coating their bodies up to their midsections. The conveyer whirred into motion and the two women moved slowly along the belt toward Kathy.

"I have to back this thing up to drop another load of chocolate on the girls. Doesn't this remind you of that movie, *The Cook, the Thief,* whatever the rest of the title is?" Kathy pressed a lever and melted chocolate came rushing down on Stephanie, covering her breasts and neck. Iris was next.

"Except in that movie the guy was baked, wasn't he?" Heaven said, trying to keep her voice even.

Kathy gave an ugly smile. "You're lucky my Courtney wasn't killed by a bread baker, Heaven. Your daughter would be toast by now."

Heaven couldn't believe this maniac was making bad food puns. "Toast, ha, ha. Good one. Why don't you let my daughter go, Kathy. She doesn't have anything to do with this. Let her go and I'll stay here in her place."

Kathy shook her head. "She's the thing you love the most, that and your restaurant. I hope I did some damage there and now I'm going to destroy your daughter. You'll see how it feels." She pulled the lever and the hot chocolate oozed out and down on Iris. Heaven searched her brain frantically for the temperature of melted chocolate but couldn't think. Was it burning the skin off Iris and Stephanie?

Both women seemed awake because they reacted to the hot chocolate as best they could, being bound. Heaven saw them tense up but she wasn't close enough to see their eyes or make eye contact. She assumed they could hear what was being said as their ears were still free of chocolate. Heaven wondered if when the chocolate covered their noses, it would close their breathing passages. The conveyer belt moved the two slowly back up the line.

"Kathy, surely there's a better way to make your point. No one will even understand why you're doing this if you don't tell the public what shits the Fosters are. They'll just think you're some nut."

"I sent a letter explaining it all to Channel Five. Mailed it yesterday. Told them how Foster's put people out of work, how they killed Courtney. They'll get it on the second after this is all over."

"When what's over?"

Kathy smiled again, jerking the belt into action. Iris and Stephanie were headed back toward the coating machine. "Look around, Heaven. See the wine bottles here on the coating machine? There are more on the conching machine and the roaster. I want to make sure the most expensive pieces of equipment are ruined. I filled them up with gasoline just like the ones I threw in your café. After the girls get coated, I'll just use my Remington to spread a little buckshot into these bottles. It should set off a nice fire."

Heaven's chest tightened. "And you want me to do what?"

"I figure you'll try to save your daughter and go up in flames with her and the Foster's bitch, here. You won't be able to run out and leave them. I know that much about you."

"Where are you going? You aren't going to be any happier after this is all over," Heaven said lamely, knowing it wasn't going to have any effect.

"Oh, yes, I will be. Revenge is sweet. I'm going to head for Montana tonight. I stole some license plates and exchanged them for my old ones. When they catch me, they catch me." With that she pulled the lever and chocolate covered Stephanie's head and shoulders. She pointed the gun at Heaven again as Iris rolled into place and the coating machine deposited hot chocolate all over her face.

Heaven couldn't help it. She started toward Kathy but didn't get far. "Stay right there," Kathy said and turned quickly and shot to her left. An explosion flamed up by the roaster. Kathy fired again. Another burst of flames. This effectively cut off one avenue of escape. Heaven was thunderstruck with the way she'd planned this out. She must have spent hours setting the place up before she snatched the two women.

Heaven looked around for the conching machine. It was about the same distance from Kathy in the opposite direction from the roaster. She saw Kathy turning toward it, then saw a blur of motion as someone leaped from behind the conveyer belt and tackled Kathy hard, bringing her down and sending the shotgun flying.

As Harold Foster rolled around on the floor with Kathy, Heaven ran over and grabbed the shotgun. She wanted to whack Kathy over the head with the butt end of the gun, but took it with her over to the conveyer belt instead and quickly wiped the chocolate off the nose and eye area of her daughter. Then she did the same with Stephanie. "Junior, where are the shop towels?" she called.

"Help," Harold said and Heaven turned, realizing that Kathy was about to get the best of him.

"It will be my pleasure," she said, and took a good swing at the side of Kathy's head with the wooden end of the shotgun. Kathy fell over like a log, stunned, her eyes rolled back in her head, but breathing. Harold sat on her, panting.

"Junior, we've got several problems here. The fire for one, getting the girls loose, and keeping Kathy from destroying us all while unconscious," Heaven said, looking around at the situation. "The girls will keep. Where's the fire extinguisher?"

At that moment the overhead sprinklers came on. Water and foam—Heaven guessed some sort of fire retardant—started pouring down. She smiled. That was one thing taken care of, hopefully.

"Moving right along," Heaven said. "Where's some rope?"

Harold was mopping the foam off his face with a hankie. "The packing wires are right over there," he said and gestured to his right.

"Perfect," Heaven said as she went over and got several of the long metal bands and handed them to Harold. "Can you get her tied up?"

Harold nodded and rolled off the semi-conscious woman, whipping the wire around her hands quickly.

Heaven moved back to the conveyer belt, but called to the man over her shoulder, "Junior, I've never been so glad to see anyone in my life. What made you come down here?" She felt for an edge of the tape on Iris's mouth. Iris's eyes were open to a squint. "Do you have a pocket knife?"

Harold reached in his pocket and pulled out a Swiss Army knife, held it out to Heaven. "We went to a friend's for dinner. Got back just after midnight and there was a message from the security company asking why my secretary had called to dismiss them. I came right down, but I just thought it was a mix-up, that they called the wrong company, until I saw the door open. Then I called 911 and snuck in the back."

Heaven cut the tape on her daughter's mouth and pulled on it. "Honey, I know this is going to hurt." She jerked it just far enough for Iris to gasp for breath. "Are you okay?" she said, tears in her eyes.

"Oh, my God, Mom. She was going to kill us."

"Hang on, sweetie. The paramedics will be here soon. Just try to relax. I'm going to take off Stephanie's tape," Heaven said, wiping chocolate off her daughter's face.

As Heaven went over to work on Stephanie, she heard the sound of sirens coming their way.

"Well, well, if this isn't a pretty picture," a voice boomed. It was Bonnie Weber, walking into the factory. "A bunch of drowned rats covered with chocolate," she said. "Mr. Foster, can you turn off the sprinklers? It looks like they did their work." The fires were smoking but seemed to be out.

Heaven smiled weakly at her friend. "Happy New Year's."

As Heaven drove down 39th Street, she couldn't believe her eyes. Dozens of Café Heaven chairs were out on the sidewalk and most of the chairs were filled. It looked like some of the guests and most of the staff had put on their coats and moved outside. Everyone had a coffee cup but Heaven was pretty sure they weren't drinking coffee. She pulled up in front and got out of the van.

Murray came rushing out. "I was staying by the phone. Is Iris okay?"

"She's down at the ER with Hank right now. I just came from there. Both she and Stephanie have third- or fourth-degree burns in some places. Hank's going to keep them all night."

She turned around to see Stuart standing in the doorway of the café. "Where is she?" he asked, looked as old as Heaven felt.

"Right down the street at the hospital. Hank's with her. She's going to be fine. It's just like a bad sunburn, Hank said."

She walked to the door and looked inside. It was a mess. The fire department had sprayed some chemicals and one table was turned over and it looked like the top had been hacked in two. She turned away and went back outside.

Murray tried to put a good spin on it. "I've already called the glass people and the insurance company. What with both the kitchen and the dining room affected, I think it'll take about a week, maybe two, to get everything back together. It could be worse," he said.

Heaven leaned up against the facade. "Yeah, it could." She turned to Stuart, who was standing on the sidewalk, looking helpless. "Stuart, I need to apologize to you. Here I've been afraid you would put my daughter in harm's way, and I did that myself. Now go down the street and be with her. Jack," she called out, "will you please drive Stuart down to the hospital? I'll be back down there in a bit."

Stuart gave Heaven a hug. "I do love her," he said. Jumpin' Jack stepped up, gave a little wave and motioned for Stuart to follow him.

"Murray, please get rid of all these people. I can't talk or be nice or even make a sentence. I've really done it this time."

Murray, not usually comfortable with physical contact, gave Heaven a clumsy embrace. "I'm proud of you. You caught the killer."

"No, she caught me. If Junior hadn't come down there, it would have been . . ." Heaven stopped in the middle of the sentence and walked into the smoky dining room. "I'll wait for the glass people. You can go on home," she said over her shoulder.

Murray followed her into the café. "We'll just bring the chairs back in," he said, trying to sound positive.

Heaven turned to him. "Look what I've done to us all. My restaurant is a shambles, we'll all be out of work for a month, my daughter was almost murdered. This is it. I've got to change my life. I've got to learn to mind my own business before I ruin everything." She sat down heavily in a dirty chair, looking around the restaurant, shaking her head. Tears trickled down her cheeks.

"It's all going to be all right, H. You'll feel better tomorrow," Murray said as he turned and went out into the cold air of the first day of a new year.